PRAISE FOR DARRELL PITT

'I found myself laughing out loud which rarely happens.'
Sondra Kerby

'An amazing book that has all the elements
of a great whodunnit.'
Ursula Sorensen

'I'm very much looking forward to reading the next book in
the series.'
Alice Hazelbaker

'This was a fun book to read. It had me laughing
a lot throughout.'
Sandy Mill

' I look forward to future installments.'
Caley Gredig

'What an awesome book!'
Michelle

BY DARRELL PITT

The Boy from Earth
Balloon Girls
A Toaster on Mars

Teen Superheroes
Book I: Diary of a Teenage Superhero
Book II: The Doomsday Device
Book III: The Battle for Earth
Book IV: The Twisted Future
Book V: Terminal Fear
Book VI: The Invisible Weapon
Book VII: The Alpha Project

Teen Superhero Bounty Hunters
Book I: Snakebite
Book II: Fear Fight
Book III: Stormfront
Book IV: Past Shadows
Book V: One Small Step

DARRELL PITT

Aliens, Apples and Murder

A ROSIE RYAN COZY MYSTERY

BOOK SIX

KENT STREET PRESS

For Cleo

1

'Spring,' I said to Trixie, 'has sprung.'

There was no doubt about it. The first day of September had arrived, and—typically for Australia—it had brought warm weather. We were out the front of Sandy's Diner, the most popular café in our beautiful little town of Cape Carson. The bay glistened in the early morning sun while seagulls flew across the calm water. Trixie, my beagle, sat at my feet as I sipped thoughtfully on my first jumbo double-shot caramel latte for the day.

Personally, I liked winter, but it could drag on a bit, and this last winter had seemed to take forever. The warm sun on my bare arms felt good. Too good. I'd end up sunburnt if I weren't careful. I peered down at the book I was reading for the next meeting of the Cape Carson Mystery Book Club. I was determined to complete it. I'd attended far too many sessions with the half-finished novel stuffed in my bag. Nothing was worse than trying to bluff that I'd read the book when faced by Wanda Gibson, the strict taskmaster of the group.

I glanced at my watch. My friend Kim Chen was joining me shortly. She'd also made the most of the first day of spring, although her idea of fun was somewhat different from mine. She'd gone out for an early morning jog and was heading home before joining me.

Kim was always telling me I needed to keep fit, and I always agreed with her. My only issue was that no one seemed to have invented a way to exercise without sweating. Exercise would be far more attractive once—

A shadow fell over me.

I glanced up to see an auburn-haired woman with a lean body. She wore a pensive expression and opened her mouth to speak. Yet no words came. It was as if she'd stopped to talk but instantly regretted it.

I know her, I thought and was annoyed with myself. Yes, I knew her. Working as a journalist with the Cape Carson Gazette for the last five years had put me in touch with thousands of people. While I remembered many of their names, there were a lot I'd known only briefly. And yet this woman...

'Rita?' I said. 'Rita Lawrence?'

Relief filled her face. 'You remember me?' she said. 'Thank goodness. I didn't want to interrupt you. I can see you're reading.'

'No. It's fine. Grab a seat.'

As the woman settled beside me, I tried to remember the last time we'd spoken. It was three years ago, and I felt myself flush with guilt. I could make a guess as to why she'd stopped.

Sandy, the diner's owner, came out and asked if Rita wanted coffee, but the woman shook her head. Rita waited until Sandy had returned inside before continuing.

'Can we talk for a minute?' Rita asked.

'Is it about your sister?' I said. 'Hailey?'

'Her case is still unsolved.'

I didn't reply because her case wasn't unsolved. Technically, there was no case. Hailey Lawrence had taken her own life. Although the events surrounding it were unusual, the decision of both the police department and the coronial inquest that had followed was that Hailey had killed herself in a fit of depression. Of course, Cape Carson was a small place, and the rumour mill had run rampant ever since her death. Stories surrounding Hailey Lawrence ranged from accident to suicide to the most diabolical theory of all—murder.

'The police investigated Hailey's death and found nothing,' I said gently. 'And a judge ruled it as suicide.'

'He was wrong.' Rita's mouth crimped into a firm line. 'Hailey wouldn't have done that. I said it then, and I say it now. She had no reason to kill herself. She had her whole life ahead of her—including a successful publishing deal on the horizon. She was even planning a trip to Europe!' Rita's voice had risen, so she swallowed and leaned forward. 'Rosie, you've had success investigating murders. You've succeeded where the police have failed. And you said there was more to Hailey's death than met the eye.'

I had said that—and regretted saying it ever since. It was one of those times when I'd shot off my mouth without thinking. I'd promised Rita that I'd continue investigating Hailey's death. And I had. For weeks, I'd looked into why Hailey would have killed herself. Then weeks bled into months. Nothing had come up in my investigation to rule out the official verdict. I'd always felt guilty about it because I'd raised Rita's hopes that Hailey hadn't killed herself.

I suppose Rita blamed herself for not recognising the signs that Hailey may have wanted to end her life.

It was unwarranted guilt. Sometimes people killed themselves, and the warning signs were not there or so well hidden as to be invisible.

My thoughts must have strayed to my face.

Rita continued. 'I'm not looking to blame anyone,' she said. 'Not you. Not anyone. It's just that everyone's given up. The cops. The legal system. Even the private investigator I hired to look into Hailey's death. He cost me a fortune and turned up nothing.'

It pained me to say my next words, but they had to be said. 'I'm not sure there's anything I can do.' A knot of discomfort filled my stomach. 'All those people have better resources than me. I'm only a reporter.'

'*Please.*' Rita said the word as if imploring a higher power, not a lowly journalist working for a coastal newspaper. 'All I'm asking is that you take another look into her death. That's all. If you don't find anything, then...' She swallowed hard. 'Then I'll give up. I'll accept that Hailey killed herself, and I'll get on with my life.' Rita took out a card with her name and number and slid it across. 'You can have access to everything the investigator discovered. Whatever you need.'

Before I could reply, Rita stood and abruptly marched off down the pavement. I was still staring after her when Kim came rushing over to the table.

'Sorry I'm late,' she said, plonking herself down. My short—some might say height-challenged—friend pushed back her cropped black hair. 'My run took a lot longer than I expected, and then I couldn't get out of the shower.' Kim peered at me. 'Why are you looking so weird?'

I explained what had transpired.

'Hailey Lawrence,' Kim said thoughtfully. 'Gosh. I haven't heard that name for years. She's the girl who jumped off the cliff?'

'*Allegedly* jumped off the cliff.'

'I remember it all seemed a bit odd.'

'More than odd.' I peered out across the bay. Despite the

spring warmth, I felt chilled. 'Hailey was in the process of signing a publishing deal that was worth a lot of money. She'd wanted to be an author since she was a kid. And then—'

'Then she killed herself,' Kim said, frowning. 'But we looked into this at the time.'

I nodded. We had investigated Hailey's death. That was over three years ago. We'd done the best we could and turned up exactly nothing. Hailey Lawrence's demise had carried all the hallmarks of suicide: a woman who suffered from anxiety with significant stress on the horizon and an easy way to end it all. To complete the picture, she'd even left a suicide note.

'True,' I said. 'But some things didn't add up.'

'Rosie, if a private investigator didn't find anything, then how will we?'

That was a good question. 'It's a different time now,' I said. 'We've got a new sergeant in charge of Cape Carson police.' Todd Parker was both a good cop and a friend. He would be far more forthcoming with information than his predecessor and more inclined to listen. 'Speaking to Sergeant Wilson about this case was like trying to communicate with a brick. He decided that Hailey killed herself and wouldn't consider any other options.'

'Then you'll look into it?'

I remembered my promise. 'Yes,' I said reluctantly. 'I don't know what I'll find, but it can't hurt to re-examine the details.'

For the first time, I noticed the bag that Kim had brought with her. 'Is that new?'

'Ah-ha!' she said, grinning. 'I was wondering when you'd notice. The bag's not the most exciting part, though. It's what's inside that counts.' Reaching in, Kim produced a good-quality Ricoh camera and a folder. 'I want to show you the results from my photography classes.'

She produced a set of eight by ten-sized prints from the folder.

'Oh great.' I tried to sound enthusiastic. As a photographer, Kim was a better librarian. She had an unerring ability to take photos of anything but the intended subject. This included pictures of elbows, the inside of her bag, and shots of the ground. One time, she'd taken over a thousand photos of the interior of a filing cabinet. I'd seen Kim's new camera, but none of her pictures. 'Well, it's nice to see that—*you've got to be kidding*!'

My eyes opened wide. Kim could barely suppress the delight on her face as she spread out the glossy prints. They were landscapes: sunsets, sunrises, and vast sweeping hills. In the foreground of one was the bay with a man pulling a fish from the water. Another was of kangaroos in a frosty field. The photos weren't good. They were *excellent*.

'Who...what...how...' I began.

'It's the classes,' she said. 'With Adrian.'

'Adrian Whiteway?' I said. She'd only briefly mentioned her friend from the photography class. Now her face turned scarlet under my gaze. 'Spill girl! Don't hold back!'

'Well, the first class was about getting to know your camera. Then the teacher moved onto lighting and framing using the rule of thirds. And then—'

I punched her arm. 'You idiot!'

'Ouch!'

'No! I want to know about the romance! Are you going out? Are you dating?'

Kim smiled. 'Kind of,' she said. 'It's not official. Nothing's happened yet. I'm going over to his place. He loves cooking and it sounds like he's good at it.'

'And he's nice?'

'He's really nice.'

I sat back and gazed at her happily. 'That's great,' I said. 'No. More than great. Magnificent.' My phone beeped, and I checked the message. 'That's Harry. He wants me to drop by the office.'

Harry Blackshore was the editor of the Cape Carson Gazette.

'I wonder what he wants,' Kim said.

'Probably something to do with AFSA.' I'd been asked to be the guest of honour at the Australian Fabric and Sewing Association conference. It was being held at a local hotel, the

Kilkenny Arms. I felt rather chuffed. The offer had come from out of the blue. Even more surprising was that my skills as a seamstress were almost non-existent. Why I'd been chosen was anyone's guess. The tailor in our family was my grandmother. 'I better get going.'

'And what about Rita Lawrence?'

I sighed. 'Can you give me a hand?'

'Of course.'

'Then we'll do what we can. Even if the news is bad, sometimes bad news is better than uncertainty. Maybe we can finally bring this whole tragic episode to an end.'

2

'It's like this,' Harry Blackshore started.

I was sitting opposite Harry in his office. It was a cramped room, stacked high with old issues of the Gazette. Although I'd been in this room a lot over the years, I'd never seen Harry look so uncomfortable.

'What is it?' I asked. 'Is something wrong?'

Harry smiled weakly. 'You'll laugh when I tell you. Really. You'll laugh.'

The way he said all this made me doubt I'd be doing much laughing. 'Harry,' I said. 'What's going on? Is it about AFSA?'

'Yes. In a strange way, it is about AFSA. And so funny about those acronyms. There are only so many to go around. Have you ever thought about that? There must be a lot of organisations with the same acronym.'

'I suppose so.' *Where is this going?* 'So what about AFSA?'

'It's amazing that so many organisations have the same acronym—'

'Harry,' I said firmly. 'What have you done?'

He forced a laugh. 'AFSA is holding its annual conference at the Kilkenny Arms,' he said. 'As you know, whenever an organisation decides to hold a conference in town, that's the place of choice. So, Natalie Cook—she's the manager there, you know—has also been caught up in this. Two organisations with the same acronym. Incredible. One is dedicated to fabric and sewing and the other...well, isn't...'

I stared at him. 'What's the other organisation?'

'The Australian Flying Saucer Association,' Harry said, shaking his head. 'Imagine that.'

'And I'm the guest of honour...' My voice trailed away. '*Not at the Flying Saucer conference?*'

Harry shrugged. 'Lucky you. Should be an interesting week.' He shuffled pages on his desk. 'Here we are. The contact is Barry Rycroft. Spoke to him on the phone earlier. Sounds like a fascinating man—'

'Harry!' I exploded. 'I can't be the guest of honour at a flying saucer conference!'

'Sure you can.'

It was like saying I could run off and scale Mount Everest in my lunchbreak.

'But...What about the Fabric and Sewing Association? My grandmother's going to the conference. She's expecting me.'

'You'll see her around. She'll be with the sewing ladies while you're with the—'

'UFO kooks.'

'Rosie, keep an open mind. And remember—you're representing the newspaper.'

'But who's covering the fabric association?'

'I've now got Jay handling them. You should have a nice few days. He'll be with the ladies, and you'll be with the...er, other people.'

'But...I don't know anything about flying saucers! I don't even believe in them!'

'You do now. I told them you were fully onboard.'

Onboard what? I wondered. *The next flight to Venus?*

He wished me well, and I marched out of his office. Doris Glow, the Gazette's receptionist, glanced up from her desk.

'Harry told you?' she said.

'Lucky me.'

'He organised it while I was in Bali,' Doris said, lowering her voice. 'Harry's a great editor but a terrible administrator.'

'I heard that!' Harry yelled from his office.

'I know!' Doris called back before turning to me. 'They're sure to be an interesting crowd. And who's to say that we're not being visited by aliens?'

It was pointless arguing. I sighed, retrieved Trixie from my office, and headed out the door. I took a deep breath. It was a beautiful day in Cape Carson, but all I could feel was disquiet.

Aliens!

There may have been aliens out there, but they sure weren't coming here. Flying saucers could all be explained away by fraud or observer error. I groaned. And now I had to spend the entire week dealing with people in tinfoil hats! And I was the guest of honour!

Grinding my teeth, I climbed into my flame red 2005 jeep and Trixie scrambled in beside me. 'How do I end up in these situations?' I asked her. 'I was once a serious journalist.'

She yowled.

'All right,' I amended. 'Not too serious. I was an entertainment reporter, but I got to deal with people who weren't as crazy as rattlesnakes. Now, look at me.'

I hit the accelerator, and we headed through town.

My phone rang as I neared the Kilkenny Arms. It was my grandmother, Nan Ryan, ringing.

'Rosie?' she said. 'I'm at the hotel, and the ladies running the show don't know anything about you.'

'Uh, yeah,' I said, pulling into the car park. I'd been speaking to Nan for several days about being the guest of honour at the Australian Fabric and Sewing Association. 'There's been a bit of a mix-up.'

'You're telling me. And there are some oddly dressed people here who don't know the first thing about stitching.'

Telling Nan I'd see her inside, I parked my jeep and went in.

The Kilkenny Arms was the most upmarket hotel in town. Set back a block from the water, it had an excellent beach view. The foyer was crowded with people who seemed firmly divided into two camps.

The first lot, all of whom seemed to be older women, congregated about in a somewhat confused clump at one end of the room. Their focus seemed to be on the other group, which appeared to outnumber them three to one. More than a few members of this other group wore t-shirts emblazoned with *The Truth is Out There* and *Become a Believer*.

Most disconcertingly were the few actually wearing tinfoil hats. There also seemed to be a lot of glitter and rainbow polyester. Had someone told me I'd wandered into a 1980's dance party, I wouldn't have been surprised.

Nan arrowed over. 'Rosie,' she said urgently. 'I've spoken to the president of AFSA, and she doesn't know anything about you being the guest of honour.'

'That's because I'm *not* the guest of honour of the sewing society,' I told her and quickly explained the mix-up. 'It looks like I'm spending the next few days with the flying saucer people.'

A figure emerged from the flying saucer group. He was a sixtyish man, stocky, with steel grey hair.

'You must be Rosie Ryan?' he said, extending a hand. 'Barry Rycroft. I'm the AFSA president.' His voice was as rough as sandpaper. 'I want to extend a warm welcome to you. The media is often biased. Most reporters want to represent us as kooks and weirdos. Such a joy to find a true believer among you.'

'Oh yes. No. I mean, it's such an honour to be here and...' I struggled to think of something to say, '...and this is my grandmother.'

Nan was unsuccessfully trying to hide a grin. 'So you're the flying saucer people,' she said. 'I once dated a man who I thought was an alien. Turned out he was Slovakian.'

Barry frowned. 'I'm not familiar with that star system.'

Nan smiled and gave me a sideways glance. 'Shame I can't drop by, Barry,' she said. 'I'm meeting with the seamstresses down the hall. You've got Rosie, though. I know she's looking forward to the conference. Been talking about it all week.'

'Thanks, Nan,' I said, deadpan.

As she headed off to join her gang, Barry gave me a reassuring smile. 'It's good to have a media member who hasn't been taken in by the government narrative.'

'Oh, uh. Yes.' It was hard to know what to say, so I continued lamely, 'I look forward to the conference.'

'Wonderful,' he said as a woman arrowed over. 'You should meet my wife, Elsa. You might know her from commercials. She's a part-time actress.'

I didn't recognise her. The woman was slim and trim with

cropped white dyed hair. Elsa smiled broadly. 'Incontinence pads,' she said.

'Sorry?'

'Those are the commercials. Shulton's Incontinence pads. I'm the woman who buys them for her grandfather. It's better than my previous job when I was the face for Hairy Harold's Motorcycles.'

'I see.'

'I'm just here to drop Barry off,' Elsa said. 'I have another conference to attend.'

'The Fabric and Sewing Association?' I said.

'No. It's the annual meeting of the Bunyip Society.'

I bit off a laugh when I saw she was serious. 'Bunyips?' The creatures were legendary monsters that haunted Australian waterholes. 'So...there are conferences about them too?'

Elsa gave me a knowing wink. 'The government hides things,' she said. 'But we know better.'

'Yep,' I sighed. 'We know better.'

She wished me well before disappearing into the crowd. 'Now come and meet some of the members,' Barry continued. 'They're an interesting bunch.' He leaned close. 'Although, I should mention that some of them are on a different wavelength. They're—how can I put it—off the planet.'

I wasn't sure if he was joking or not, but I trailed after him to a small breakaway group.

'Our two committee members,' Barry began, introducing a tall man with thinning red hair and big eyes. 'Jasper Kidwell, our club treasurer. His specialty is electronics.'

'You're doing the audio visuals for the conference?'

'Oh no,' Jasper said. 'I did all that when I was a teenager. Many years ago, now. I listen to frequencies from space, trying to hear extra-terrestrial messages.'

'Really?' It sounded interesting. 'What does that sound like?'

'Hmm. Static, mostly.'

Oh great.

He continued. 'Although, I've had some interesting transmissions,' he said. 'One night, I was sure I could hear the words *Area 51 marmalade jam*. It went on for hours.'

'Area 51 marmalade jam?' I repeated. 'What does it mean?'

'No idea. Not unless aliens were after a recipe to take back to their home world. Another time they transmitted *Eskimo arm take granite*. I have no idea what that means either.'

'Beats me,' I said, honestly. 'And that's from listening to static?'

'It takes an expert,' Jasper informed me soberly. 'People can easily mistake static for words.'

'I can imagine.'

'We know they're coming here. Sometimes they direct their messages at certain individuals they want to communicate with.'

'The visitors?'

He raised an eyebrow. 'The aliens who are visiting Earth.'

'Oh, yes. Of course.'

'I'm also busy flying drones. Not only are drones a great hobby, but I use them to monitor the area around my farm.' He leaned close. 'You've got to keep an eye out.'

He gave me a knowing look, although I had no idea what I was supposed to know. Was he keeping an eye out for UFO's? Aliens? Or government agents?

Before I could voice my confusion, however, a young woman appeared at my elbow.

'At last,' she said. The newcomer was a squat girl with pink hair and a nose ring who looked like she should have been in high school. She wore sunglasses, a bomber jacket, and a baseball cap. 'So good to have you here, Rosie. We need true believers like you in the media. Most journalists treat us like we're a bunch of kooks.'

'And your name is?' I asked.

'Neo. I'm the AFSA secretary.'

'Neo?' What kind of name was that? 'You mean like from The Matrix?'

'The movies only got it partly right.' Somehow she seemed to speak without barely moving her lips. 'The universe is a construct built within a four-dimensional inversion.'

Jasper sighed. 'We don't agree on everything,' he said. 'I just think aliens are coming from other worlds. It's a simpler explanation.'

'And I'm more sold on time travel,' Barry piped up. 'I think they're us, but from the future. They don't want to interfere with the past. Altering history is dangerous. At the same time, they're keen to know us. Understand how we operate.'

'But if they're human...' I started. 'Don't a lot of aliens have grey skin? Or look like reptiles?'

'Probably horribly mutated from genetic wars.'

'I see.' I turned back to the girl. 'Do you have any other name?'

She shook her head wearily. 'It's best if I don't share it,' she said. 'I've attempted—shall we say *software incursions*—into the CIA, FBI, and every other big government security agency. The more anonymous I am, the longer I can operate without being tracked by authorities.'

This took a moment to sink in. 'You're a hacker?' I said. 'Goodness. And you hack into government agencies? What have you gotten into?'

'So far, not much. It's harder to get in than I expected. I did send a *very* nasty email to the Bureau of Meteorology.' Shaking her head, she chuckled. 'That showed them. Anyway, I never share my real name. The government's watching us twenty-four-seven.' She lowered her voice. 'I think there's a real chance the prime minister isn't human.'

'A few people have wondered that.'

At that moment, I spotted someone from the corner of my eye. Excusing myself, I pushed through the crowd.

'Jay?' I said.

Jay Patel was my fellow reporter. He smiled brightly at me.

'Rosie!' he said. 'Harry told me you're a celebrity this week.'

'Yeah. Sure. That's me all right: a B-grade celebrity.' I quickly explained the mix-up in organisations. 'So you're covering the Fabric and Sewing Association?'

'They seem like a nice group. They're old, though. I don't think anyone's under the age of eighty.'

Jay looked pleased, and I could understand why. Much of what he did for the Gazette was rewrite press releases and handle sport for the paper. 'Yes, I'm sure,' I said. 'Make certain you get plenty of pictures. You know what Harry always says.'

'Pictures, pictures, pictures?'

'You got it.'

Barry Rycroft angled over with a sheet of paper. 'Rosie,' he said. 'I've got a copy of your itinerary here. I'm not sure if Harry gave it to you. He seemed a bit confused when I spoke to him.'

I scanned the page.

Although plenty of free time was scheduled, there were also lots of sessions with quirky-sounding names like *Is the Moon*

Hollow? and *When will JFK return?* I wasn't required to attend them all, but the sessions they had me down for were still bad enough. Maybe now was a good time to fake a heart attack. 'That's Harry,' I said, nodding. 'Confused. Can you tell me what the session *Dealing With Trans-dimensional Portals* is about?'

'Alien encounters can be frightening,' Barry said. 'Sometimes people wake up to find an alien has entered through a trans-dimensional portal: essentially a gap in time and space. We talk people through the process of dealing with such a surprise.'

I sighed.

I'm sure you do.

3

'Rosie Ryan!' Todd Parker said brightly. 'What brings you to my humble office?'

The police sergeant was hunched behind his desk. It was morning, and I'd interrupted him during one of his marathon typing sessions.

I thought of them as marathons because Todd, for all his incredible assets, was the slowest typist I'd ever encountered. More than once, I'd felt the violent urge to shoulder him out of the way so I could dive in and finish his report.

'Does the name Hailey Lawrence mean anything to you?' I asked.

'Should it?'

I sat down opposite as Trixie settled onto the floor at my feet. I slipped her a homemade doggy snack.

'Hailey died almost three and a half years ago,' I told him. 'Suicide, supposedly.'

Todd nodded, thinking. 'I remember now,' he said. 'I've had

her sister in here a few times.'

'Rita Lawrence?'

'She thinks that Hailey's death wasn't suicide. It could have been murder?'

'That's the theory.'

The big police officer sat back in his seat. He was built like a real-life version of The Hulk. 'It all happened long before I started here,' he said. 'That was back in Peter Wilson's time. Hailey Lawrence lived on the Great Coastal Road? I recall she suffered from depression and jumped off a cliff?'

'That's the official story.'

'There was something about a boyfriend?'

'Not a boyfriend.'

This was slightly frustrating. I knew more about this case than Todd, although I suppose that was expected. He'd only been in Cape Carson for six months, and I'd been here five years.

'Owen Stamett and Hailey Lawrence were friends,' I said. 'They belonged to the same writing group. There was a lot of talk about Owen being fixated with Hailey. About a month after she died, he disappeared.'

'When you say disappeared...'

'Off the face of the Earth. His bank accounts have never been accessed, and he's never contacted his family. Although there's been reported sightings of him over the years, none have ever been confirmed. He's currently listed as a missing person.'

Todd stroked his chin. 'So the guy who was fixated with Hailey went missing soon after she 'allegedly' killed herself. I'm assuming the theory is he killed her and disappeared to escape the law.'

'Or also took his own life. Phone records trace his last known location to Elk's Gap, where his phone pinged off towers. From there, he simply disappeared off the planet.'

'I can check the old files if you like,' Todd said. 'But you know what you should do? See Peter Wilson. You can't beat getting a firsthand account.'

I sighed. 'Sergeant Wilson and I never saw eye-to-eye.'

'I know he was an irascible old grouch. He's retired now. Lives down at Briar Lake. I'm sure he'd speak to you.'

Despite Todd's optimism, I wasn't so sure. Peter Wilson and I had crossed swords on many occasions. I hadn't thought much of him as a cop, and he hadn't appreciated my helping with cases.

More than once, he'd referred to my help as interfering!

The nerve of the man!

'I can ring ahead if you like,' Todd offered.

'That could be handy,' I admitted. 'Although I'm not sure how helpful he'll be.'

Todd shrugged. 'You never know.'

I told him I was free Thursday afternoon, and Todd said he'd see what he could arrange. He got me to wait in reception. It was fifteen minutes later when Todd appeared.

'It took some doing,' he said. 'But Peter Wilson will talk to you.'

'Bet he's looking forward to it.'

Todd stifled a grin. 'He did get kind of excited when I mentioned your name,' he said. 'But probably not the kind of excited you'd want. Several words he used about you I won't repeat. Anyway, I reminded him that Owen was still missing and no one was actively working the case. He's got nothing to lose by talking to you.'

I thanked Todd and was about to head off when he stopped me.

'By the way,' he said. 'Interested in dinner one night?'

My heart gave a tiny leap, but I tried not to look excited. Todd and I had never been a couple, and I had almost given up on anything happening. He'd had an old school friend named Yvonne staying with him for a while. Or, at least, she was *supposed* to be an old school friend.

Before Yvonne had appeared on the scene, I would have jumped at the chance of an intimate dinner. Now I felt a tinge of unease. While I didn't want to appear desperate, I also didn't want to drive him away.

'Kim's been talking about holding a dinner party,' I said. 'Maybe I can push her along.'

'Okay,' Todd said slowly. 'Can she cook?'

'Sure she can.'

'Food that's edible I mean.'

Kim had an uneven track record when it came to her culinary skills. One night she'd cooked us a curry so hot that we almost passed out.

'She's got a new boyfriend,' I said. 'Apparently, he can cook up a storm.'

'Sounds great.'

After I thanked him again, Trixie and I returned to my car. It was afternoon. Fortunately, I didn't have to deal with any more UFO people for the day. The main event wouldn't begin until tomorrow, so I rang Rita Lawrence.

'Rosie!' she said. 'I'm so glad you've rung. Are you going to look into Hailey's case?'

'I will,' I said cautiously. The woman sounded so relieved that I instantly felt guilty. 'But I can't make any promises. Maybe nothing will turn up. Or maybe something got missed. You said I could examine the report from the private investigator?'

'Absolutely.'

I thought for a moment. 'Do you mind if I bring my friend Kim?' I asked. 'You might remember her. She can be quite helpful.'

Rita said that was fine. I told her I'd be over later and then rang Kim.

'Sure, I'm free,' Kim said after I explained what I was doing. 'Rita and Hailey's place was on the Coastal Road? Down near Hansom Bay? A drive along the coast would do me the world of good.'

'Will that be fine with your work?'

'I've got some things to do, but I can see to them later. Someone's on leave, so I've got to be here tonight anyway.'

Soon, I'd picked Kim up from the library, and we were making our way down the coast. The sun was getting low on the horizon, and the cliff face was filling with shadows. The ocean on our right was calm, and the sky clear.

'It's beautiful out there,' Kim said.

'Hard to beat.'

Trixie barked in agreement.

We soon reached Hansom Bay and pulled onto a road leading up the escarpment. Now we were here, a sense of disquiet had begun forming in my gut. I'd come this way a lot when Rita's sister had died. Seeing the same sights reminded me of how remiss I'd been. While I'd gotten on with my life, Rita had been struggling to understand her sister's death.

Well, I thought. *I'm here now.*

About a kilometre from the coast, we passed a letterbox and drove down a winding driveway. The old timber farmhouse sat in a narrow valley with a hill rising sharply behind. Daffodils were scattered across the front yard. A rusting farm hoe lay abandoned on one side of the house. On the other sat a beaten-up ute. A miniature wishing well, surrounded by azaleas, sat silent and derelict.

I stopped the car.

'We're back,' Kim said.

'I didn't think it would be this hard,' I admitted.

'You can't blame yourself,' Kim said. 'We did what we could.'

'Shame it wasn't enough.'

I felt like restarting the engine and driving off. Maybe I would have even done it, except the front door opened at that moment, and Rita appeared. I reluctantly got out of the jeep with Kim and Trixie in my wake.

'Thanks for coming,' Rita said.

'You remember Kim?' I said.

'Of course. Come on inside, and I'll show you the report from the private investigator.'

We followed her into the house, where Rita led us to the living room. It was still as I remembered it. Neat. Orderly. Magazines on the coffee table. Van Gogh prints on the wall. A new addition was a photo of Hailey on the mantlepiece. Lean, with auburn hair like her sister, Hailey had a kind of wild beauty. In the picture, she was smiling, as if ready to burst into laughter.

Rita handed us the investigator's report. The first thing I noticed was the logo on the front page.

'Gerald Lime Investigations,' I read.

'You know him?' Rita said.

'We've met Gerry once before.'

'What did you think?'

'He seemed competent.'

'Then I'll leave you to it. I'll be in the garden if you need me.'

Kim and I sat down to read. It took almost twenty minutes to examine the report from front to back. When I finally laid down the pages, I felt more than a little depressed. Gerry Lime had looked into the same angles as us: Hailey's actions in the days before her death, the suicide note, autopsy, and Owen Stamett's later disappearance. Gerry's investigation was not only more comprehensive than that conducted by Kim and me, but it deepened my suspicion that Hailey had not killed herself.

'He's done good work,' Kim muttered, putting down her pages. 'Better than us.'

'Better than the police, too,' I added.

Kim picked up the report and read aloud. '*Hailey made several purchases in the days before she supposedly killed herself. She bought three books, a new dress, and cosmetics.*'

'Gerry also checked her browser history,' I added. 'She searched for new cars and European holidays.'

'Those are hardly the actions of someone planning to take their own life.' Kim hesitated. 'Her internet searches couldn't have been research for her book?'

'I doubt it,' I said. 'The book was almost done and dusted. The publisher had supplied her with a contract, and the first round of editing had been scheduled.' I shook my head. 'No. This had nothing to do with research. And there's no indication that Hailey was working on another book.' I scanned the pages. 'And Gerry makes a good point about the suicide note.'

'That always seemed fishy.'

Hailey had supposedly typed the note on her laptop. Then she'd printed it and left the page on her desk. Most people handwrote suicide notes and made personal remarks to their loved ones.

'*I can't take the stress any longer,*' I read. '*It's too much for me.*' I stopped. I'd read the same words three years before, and they hadn't rung true then either. 'There's no mention of her sister. Friends. Regrets. Nothing.' My gut churned. *It doesn't make sense.* Rita had been right all along. 'Hailey was murdered and her death staged to look like suicide.'

4

'Let's look at where she died,' I said.

'We've seen it before.'

'I need to see it again.'

Rita was outside, digging in the garden. When I asked if we could return to where Hailey took her life, she pointed at the hill behind the house. 'You probably remember the way,' she said. 'I don't go up there anymore. It's too hard.'

'I understand,' I said.

Kim, Trixie, and I started up the steep trail. We weren't far from the coast, and a stiff onshore breeze flowed inland. It was spring, and the sun was warm on our faces, yet I felt chilled.

I remembered climbing this hill three years ago when there was a worn track on the hillside. Both Rita and Hailey had come up this way a lot. It was understandable; the view from the top was breathtaking. Now the path was rough and over-grown. No one had been up here for years. I wondered why Rita even stayed in the house.

Maybe because it still connects her to Hailey, I thought.

Reaching the crest of the hill, the breeze hit us hard. Below us lay a ravine and another hill on the other side. Beyond that, out of sight lay the road and the ocean beyond. We crept to the edge and peered into the crevasse. It was all rocks and weeds down there. A fall from here would kill anyone.

Someone could stumble over the side if they weren't careful. It was an impressive view and an equally impressive drop. If this were a public lookout, there'd be fencing and warning signs. But this was private property. Probably Rita and Hailey had been up here hundreds of times. In the old days. Before everything went wrong.

I peered down again. I didn't want to think about what it would be like. Standing here at the top with someone you trusted. And then they gave you one good shove, and then you were flying through the air, knowing what awaited you at the bottom. One of the crime scene pictures had been in Gerry Lime's folder. Hailey's body was an untidy shape at the bottom, like a sheet from a clothesline set adrift by the wind.

'She must have known her killer,' I said.

'Or she could have been carried up here, unconscious,' Kim said. 'And her body dumped over the side. A single head injury probably wouldn't be noticed by the coroner.'

I peered doubtfully down the trail we'd climbed. 'That's quite a hill,' I said. 'Carrying someone up wouldn't be easy.'

'You'd have to be strong,' Kim agreed, biting her lip. 'The police didn't find anything unusual up here. No sign of a struggle.'

'Any evidence would be swept away by the wind in seconds.'

Kim glanced back down at the house. 'I wonder if Rita's kept many of Hailey's belongings.'

'Let's find out.'

Returning to the farmhouse, we found Rita in the living room, listlessly watching a gameshow on television.

'I haven't changed Hailey's room,' Rita said when we asked. 'Just in case there were clues in there.'

I wasn't sure what could have been missed after three years. 'In the report, Gerry says he searched Hailey's room,' I said. 'He didn't note anything in particular.'

Rita hesitated. 'There was something that didn't make it into the report,' she said. 'I didn't say anything because it was more a gut feeling than anything else. I didn't want to sound paranoid.'

'What is it?' Kim asked.

'Do you remember me saying that I thought someone had rummaged through Hailey's belongings?'

Rita had told us that three years before. We nodded.

'Well,' she said. 'It wasn't just her room. I didn't realise it for a few weeks. Even months. But someone had gone through the whole house. It was little things. Drawers slightly askew.

Clothing not quite in its place. Books out of order. I'd seen it in her room, but I thought that was because the police had been there.'

'Was anything missing?' Kim asked.

'Does the contents of her computer count?'

I nodded, remembering. This had come up in the original investigation. 'It had been wiped,' I said.

'They'd even tried to delete the backup. Fortunately, it's not easy to get rid of that stuff.'

The police had offered an explanation for the missing files. 'Sergeant Wilson put that down to Hailey's state of mind. That she was unwell and wanted to purge her life.'

Rita's bottom lip quivered. 'Hailey didn't kill herself,' she said. 'The killer was looking for something.'

'Was there anything...incriminating in her files?' I asked.

'Not that I could see.'

'We'll take a look in Hailey's room.'

Rita led us upstairs. Pushing the door open was like stepping back into the past. It hadn't changed. Not in the three years since Hailey had died. Hailey had not just been a writer but a reader as well. One whole wall was taken up with a bookcase, stuffed to overflowing with an assortment of authors. There didn't seem any logic to it. Her love of books extended to her desk. More books were piled here beside a laptop. The device looked dated now, although it would have once been top of the range.

Another wall was covered with file cards. I remembered these from years before. They had been notes for her book. I took a closer look. Stuck amidst these was a printout of the acceptance email from the publisher. I read the first few words.

We are pleased to inform you that...

I sighed. That must have been one of the greatest moments of Hailey's life. I'd tried writing a few books myself, but they never went further than chapter three. A shelf over her desk was stacked with ornaments. Looked like she was a Sailor Moon fan. There were statues of the characters from the anime show. Among them sat a red, shining plastic apple.

I know what that's from, I thought. *The writing group that Hailey belonged to.*

Both Owen and Hailey were members of the same writing club. The group had met once a month until Hailey's death. Her passing—and Owen's subsequent disappearance—had spelled the club's end.

I touched one figure. No dust. Rita obviously cleaned in here regularly. This could almost be the room of someone who's gone out for the day.

'What happened to Hailey's book?' Kim asked. 'After she died?'

Rita grimaced. 'That was yet another tragedy,' she said. 'I thought the release of her book would bring some peace. At least that would live on after her. But it wasn't to be. The contract hadn't been signed with the publisher, and they could pull out at any time. With Hailey dead, they weren't prepared to proceed to the editing stage without her and withdrew their offer.' She paused. 'Even though I tried approaching a few publishers after that, none of them showed any interest in the novel.'

'It was a vampire book?' I said.

'*The Second Death of Reginald Tanner*,' Rita said. 'A story about a guy who is bitten by a vampire in 1915. He lives through the next century of world events, getting an insight into life—and death.'

'Vampire novels are often popular,' Kim said.

'Their success comes and goes. At least, that's what the publisher said.'

A digital photo frame sat on the desk, the screen blank. I picked it up. 'Does this work?'

'I turned it off because it was chewing up electricity,' she said and snapped the power back on. It flickered for a moment before an image appeared of Hailey and Rita. 'Even when Hailey was alive, she didn't like this thing going. Said it was a waste of natural resources.'

The images scrolled from one to the next until one came up of Hailey with a group of people. They were an eclectic bunch and vaguely familiar.

'Those are the members of Plastic Apple,' Rita said.

I nodded. 'Hailey's writing group,' I said. 'They met monthly?'

'Hailey was the youngest member of the group. She work-shopped her novel with them and was grateful for their help. They stopped meeting after her death.'

The images continued to carousel from one to the next. When the picture of the Plastic Apple members arrived again, I peered a little more closely. 'That's Owen Stamett,' I said. 'You think he killed Hailey?'

The woman hesitated. 'I don't know what to believe,' she said. 'He had an almost unhealthy fixation with her. You know Hailey was a beautiful woman. A lot of men were attracted to her. Only thing is, though, that Hailey was chronically shy and found it hard to speak to people. And Owen was older. Hailey was only twenty-two. Owen was thirty. You recall he disappeared soon after Hailey died?'

'Three years ago, you thought he was the main suspect,' I said.

'Yes.' The word hung in mid-air. 'Now I'm not so sure.'

'What changed your mind?' Kim asked.

'I bumped into Owen's father a few months back. You know what it's like in a small town. Sooner or later, you bump into everyone. Anyway, we had a heated discussion—some might call it argument—about his son. He swore blind that Owen had nothing to do with Hailey's death. That he hadn't seen or heard of Owen in all that time.' Rita bit her lip. 'Then he said something weird. He said their house had been broken into after Owen's disappearance. Nothing had been taken, but things were out of place.'

Three years before, I had thought Owen could have been responsible for killing Hailey. Unfortunately, Owen's father had refused to speak to us. His reluctance—and Peter Wilson's stonewalling—had killed our investigation.

Rita left Kim and me to search the room. We spent the next few minutes going through Hailey's belongings. I was mindful that we had done an almost identical search three years ago and turned up nothing.

Standing in the centre of the room, I peered around the space, wondering if we'd missed anything. My eyes settled on Hailey's desk. It was still stacked high with books and papers. I went through the documents and found nothing. They were primarily loose notes for her novel. A lot of information about vampires and myths relating to monsters.

Kim had been watching me. 'What about behind the desk?' she asked. 'Papers are always falling behind my desk at work.'

Leaning over to peer down the back, I spotted nothing at first. Then I realised there was a folded page that had fallen into the gap. Kim helped me to drag the piece of furniture forward.

I opened the page. The words on it had been printed using

a computer. It read:

I'm sick of playing your silly games.

Stop this, or you'll be sorry.

'If that isn't a threatening letter,' Kim said, 'then I don't know what is.'

I turned the page over. 'There's no sign who sent it,' I said. 'Or even if it was sent. It seems unlikely, but Hailey could have written this.'

I popped the sheet into a plastic envelope for safekeeping. Then Kim and I took a few pictures of the room, including the photo in the digital frame of Plastic Apple, before returning downstairs. I showed Rita the note.

'Hailey would never write this,' she said, her eyes narrowing. 'Someone threatened Hailey, probably the same person who killed her.'

'We don't know that for sure,' I said. 'I'll hand this over to the police. They may be able to fingerprint it.'

'This could lead to Hailey's killer!' Rita said, gripping my arm.

I didn't want to raise her hopes, although finding the note was a step in the right direction. 'I'll be looking into this further,' I said, all too aware that I'd made an identical promise before, and it had led to nothing. 'I don't know where this will lead, but we'll do what we can.'

Rita thanked us for our efforts. She stayed in the doorway

and watched us leave as we drove away.

'What now?' Kim asked.

Trixie whined as I considered.

'I'll take this note to Todd,' I said. 'We also need to speak to Owen Stamett's father.' I stopped. 'But not until tomorrow. First, I've got to deal with some aliens.'

Kim stared at me. 'What do you mean?'

I told her about the mix-up with AFSA, and that I had somehow become the guest of honour.

Her eyes opened wide. 'That's...*fantastic*!'

'Huh?'

'Are you kidding?' Her face was flushed with excitement. 'I saw a flying saucer when I was a kid! It was incredible! I heard about the UFO conference. I wanted to go, but I knew you'd think I was crazy!'

I groaned. 'Kim,' I said. 'Don't tell me you believe in all this UFO stuff.'

'Believe? Don't you?'

'I don't believe in anything I can't see with my own eyes,' I grumbled.

'Well, I've seen one. It went streaking across the sky when I was twelve. I was on a picnic in the country with my parents when I saw it. Big silver thing it was. It hovered on the horizon for a moment and then went—*zoosh* across the sky.'

'It couldn't have been a plane? Or a bird?'

'Or Superman? Seriously, Rosie, did you not hear me? It went *zoosh*!'

'Was it *zoosh* or more like *zooooosh*!'

She punched my arm. 'Now you're being silly,' she said. 'Rosie, you *must* let me come along.'

'Let you come along? Are you kidding? I need all the help I can get.' I fixed her with a stare. 'But don't do anything silly. Don't come dressed as an astronaut.'

'I only did that for book week at the library.' She sighed happily. 'Flying saucers. Aliens. Outer space. What more could a girl ask for?'

5

'...and I'd like to introduce this year's guest of honour to the AFSA conference.' Barry Rycroft was speaking. 'Rosie Ryan is a local journalist with the Cape Carson Gazette. She worked as an entertainment reporter for various Melbourne newspapers before moving to Cape Carson. Most reporters are just media puppets, but Rosie's a true believer, and we're lucky to have her here.'

The audience responded with a smattering of applause.

I was sitting at the front desk with the three members of the AFSA committee and feeling more than a small sense of dismay. There were about fifty people squeezed into the room. Some were old. Some were young. Many gazed back at me with expressions ranging from curiosity to hostility. The only smiling face in the audience belonged to Kim. For her attendance, at least, I was grateful. It would have been awful going through this whole experience alone.

A man at the back cautiously raised a hand. 'We couldn't get the Minister for Defence?' he called.

'No,' Barry said.

'Minister for Foreign Affairs?'

'No.'

'The Minister for Sport?'

'No.'

'How about Hugh Jackman?'

'I wanted him.' It was pink-haired Neo who spoke up. She was sitting beside me. 'He's one of the few celebrities who hasn't been replaced.' Neo clenched her fists. 'Saddest day of my life was when they swapped out Ryan Reynolds.'

Jasper shook his head in frustration. 'It's not replacements we've got to worry about,' he said firmly. 'It's plain old alien invasions. We can be invaded at any moment. We've got to be prepared.'

Several audience members spoke at once, and Barry raised his hand for order. 'All this can be discussed later at the appropriate time,' he said. 'Our session today is about life in nearby star systems, and how likely it is that they're visiting.'

An elderly woman raised her hand. 'Will you be covering cross-stitch?' she asked. 'I've never been able to do that.'

'That's down the hall,' Barry explained.

She got up and toddled out.

'Now let's look at our nearest star system,' Barry continued. 'Proxima Centauri. How likely is it that Centaurians are visiting Earth?'

'Ridiculous!' a man proclaimed from the back row.

Neo sat forward. 'What makes you say that?'

'They don't have faster than light travel.'

And so the morning wore on. Being the guest of honour of such an event meant sitting still and appearing interested. It wasn't easy. They didn't need me in attendance. A cardboard version of me would have sufficed. The hardest part was feigning attention. My mouth muscles were frozen in a constant state of earnest engagement, an expression caught somewhere between a frown and a glare.

Botox was *definitely* a possibility after this.

I wondered if I could bring earphones to the next session and listen to music while they argued about what aliens were visiting earth and how they were getting here.

The whole discussion was so outlandish that I only just managed to stay awake. Finally, the morning session ended, and everyone got up for lunch.

Stretching, I wondered if I could fake a family emergency when Kim approached.

'You did very well,' she said, smiling. 'You almost looked interested.'

'Really? I did my best. At one point I thought an embolism was coming on.' I sidled close to her. 'I'm completely out of my depth.'

'Don't worry,' Kim said. 'I'm an expert on flying saucers. I've been watching the skies ever since I saw that flying saucer.'

'Really? You must have a sore neck.'

Kim laughed. 'There's a lot of hokeyness out there,' she admitted. 'If you go too far down the rabbit hole, you end up on a search for Atlantis.'

'I find it hard enough to find the lady's bathroom.'

We headed off to lunch and had just sat in the restaurant when a bunch of older women came pouring into the room.

'Rosie!' Nan called. She came bustling over, her gaze fixing on Kim. 'Goodness, Kim. What are you doing here?'

'Rosie invited me. I love anything to do with UFOs. I saw one when I was a kid.'

At that moment, Jay Patel also entered, and I waved him over. As we all settled around the table, they asked me how I was finding the UFO conference.

'It's fine,' I said diplomatically. 'Everyone thinks I'm a true believer. They don't know I'm a cynical old grouch.' I turned to Jay. 'What are your thoughts on the subject?'

'On UFOs and aliens?' Jay said. 'I'm sure there's life out there. Lots of it. Our own Milky Way galaxy has around three hundred billion stars, and it's been estimated that there are about a trillion galaxies. There's either extra-terrestrial life out there or it's an extremely lonely universe.'

I sighed. 'You should be the one attending the flying saucer conference, and I should be with the textile ladies.'

'Jay's having a wonderful time,' Nan said, patting his hand. 'Our secretary didn't turn up, so we've got him taking minutes.'

'Really?' I turned to him. 'You're all right with that?'

'Um. They threatened to throw me out if I didn't agree.'

'Those old ladies are a tough bunch.'

'It's a shame I didn't end up at your conference.' He nodded to Nan. 'No offense. I'm quite interested in alien life.'

'Okay,' I sighed. 'So why haven't they contacted us? Why haven't we been overrun with aliens?'

'They may not be coming here and I'll tell you why. First, life on alien worlds could be microbes or algae, so they're not capable. Second, with our current technology, it can take thousands of years to travel to other star systems. They may have the same problem. And finally, it's possible that they haven't evolved at the same time as us. Considering that the universe is thirteen billion years old, they may have evolved a million years ago and wiped themselves out in a nuclear war.'

Kim chimed in. 'Or they consider us so primitive that we're not worthwhile speaking to,' she said. 'It would be like someone trying to communicate with an ant.'

'Okay,' I nodded. 'Fair enough.'

'Or they could already be here.' Kim glanced around and lowered her voice. 'And the government knows about them.

I've heard there's a place in the outback called Zone Nine where they're holding the remains of alien bodies and a space-ship. They're supposedly working out their science so we can have faster than light travel.'

'Kim,' I groaned. 'Whoever heard of Zone Nine?'

'I've heard of it,' Jay said.

'Me too,' Nan said.

I was astonished. 'What?'

'There was a documentary on the history channel.'

I rolled my eyes. 'So it must be true.'

Our food arrived, and we ate. After lunch, I was heading back to the meeting room when Barry approached.

'Rosie, I realise we haven't introduced you to Laniakea.'

I had met no one by that name. 'No, I haven't met him,' I said, 'or her.'

'Ha!' Barry chortled. 'It sounds like you haven't brushed up on your large-scale structures of the universe.'

The book I was currently reading was entitled *The Clue of the Unlit Candle* which, so far, had included no mention of large-scale universal structures. Although, it did contain a fascinating mystery surrounding a locked trunk from which a man had vanished into thin air.

Barry motioned me after him. Since the earlier session, members of the UFO society had carried in a ping-pong table supporting something that looked like an enormous piece of abstract art. Spanning two by three metres, the object had been made with tiny Lego pieces. Many thousands, by the look of it. The structure vaguely resembled the neurons that would span out across the brain or an elaborate underwater coral construction. It sat daintily balanced on the table.

'My goodness,' I said. 'What is that?'

'Laniakea. It's a model showing the galaxies in our super-cluster. It represents most of the whole universe and contains an estimated one hundred thousand galaxies.' Barry pointed to a small filament branching off from one side. 'The Milky Way, our home, is over here.'

'It's incredible.' I was impressed, although I couldn't quite fathom the size. 'So how big is this? The real version, I mean.'

'Around five hundred million lightyears across.'

'And a lightyear is the distance travelled by light in a year?' I said. 'That's big. And who built it?'

'Half a dozen AFSA volunteers. Took them a year.'

'This must be the highlight of the conference.'

Barry bit his lip. 'Actually,' he said, 'there is something even more impressive. I've brought the Blackwood relic with me.'

Goodness, I thought. *How incredible that would be—if only I knew what it was!*

'I'm not familiar with it,' I confessed.

'It's one of the only pieces of a flying saucer ever recovered in Australia,' Barry explained. 'The society purchased it years ago, and it's been in my safekeeping ever since. I don't bring it to all the conferences for security reasons. It's too valuable.' He drew himself up. 'I think of myself as *The Keeper of the Relic*.'

I did my best to look impressed. 'Goodness.' I nodded to the Laniakea model. 'Do you mind if I take some pictures?'

'Please do.' Barry looked pleased. 'I can take one of you with the supercluster behind you.'

After snapping a few shots, I handed Barry my phone and went to the display to pose. I leaned against the table. 'How does this look?' I asked.

He lined up the image. 'Pretty good. Maybe lean back a little.'

I leaned back, putting my hands on the edge of the table. Something moved. There was a splintering crack, and I heard something sliding behind me. Turning, I saw the middle of the ping-ping table separating. Almost in slow motion, the delicate model seemed to fall in on itself as I toppled backward onto the collapsing table.

Cra-ash!

Lego exploded in all directions. It was like a bomb going off with tiny shrapnel flying everywhere. The expression on Barry's face was one of pure horror. He even dropped my phone in shock. By then, I was on the floor, sitting in an untidy mess of shattered table and Lego blocks.

I had a reputation for clumsiness. I'd knocked over clothing displays. Slid down stairs. Stepped on dresses. Fallen off chairs.

But I'd never destroyed most of the known universe in one fell swoop.

Jasper and Neo came charging into the room, followed by dozens of members of the flying saucer society. Someone screamed. Another person fainted. A couple snapped pictures. The crowd gathered around as I picked myself up from amidst the debris. They seemed unable to speak, the shock of the destruction being so extreme.

I had to say something. 'I...leaned against the table,' I said, swallowing. 'I barely touched it.'

Fortunately, Neo came to my rescue. 'Government agents,' she growled. 'It's gotta be.'

'Yep,' I agreed, swallowing. 'Gotta be.'

6

'Rubbish!' Bert Stamett snapped. 'Total rubbish!'

It was the next day, and Kim, Trixie and I were sitting in the living room of the old man's home. It was an old farmhouse nestled into the hillside ten kilometres from the coast. The gardens around the weatherboard home were overgrown, with giant eucalyptus surrounding the building. The house itself was painted blue and red. Maybe it had seemed a good idea while perusing the local hardware store. In practice, it just made the building look tacky.

Bert was a thin, tall man who smoked and drank too much. The house reeked of stale tobacco and spilt beer. It was hard to associate this man with his son. Although I'd never met Owen Stamett, I'd seen photos of him. Owen was well-built and strong. He'd been in the army for a short time before becoming a cop for an even shorter time.

During the initial investigation, Bert had refused to see us. I suppose, at the time, he was fighting off allegations from all sides. The news story we'd run with at the time was that Owen had gone missing. It was Rita who'd raised the possibility that her sister had been murdered by him. The mention of that in one of our articles had been enough to make Bert refuse our calls.

Even now, he might have slammed the door in our face if not for Trixie. She had a beguiling effect on people, encouraging them to open their doors and mouths. Trixie had helped me to land difficult interviews on more than one occasion.

We were settled on the edge of oversized lounge chairs that seemed unpleasantly sticky. 'Those allegations were raised years ago,' I said. 'We're just following up to find out what happened to both Owen and Hailey. I'm sure you'd like to know.'

'Of course,' he said. 'Owen was my son. Disappeared off the face of the earth. Murdered, I reckon.'

'Were Owen and Hailey close?' I asked.

'Not really,' he said. 'They were both members of that writing club. What was it called? Plastic Spoon?'

'Plastic Apple,' Kim said.

'That's the one. Owen had an idea in his head that he would be a writer. He wrote those...what do you call them...fantasy books? Men in their underwear waving swords around.' Bert shook his head. 'He had thousands of pages written. Did nothing with it. He should have stuck to being a cop. He was good at that.'

'Why did he leave the police force?' I asked.

Bert hesitated and looked away. For a moment, I thought he would refuse to answer, but then he gave a slight nod. 'I might as well tell you,' he said. 'Owen had a bad temper. He argued with a suspect. More than an argument. A teenager, high on drugs, headbutted him during an arrest. Things got out of hand back at the station, and the teenager got his arm broken.'

'This wasn't in Cape Carson,' I said.

I would have known about it.

'No. It was Melbourne. That's after he left the army.'

'And what happened there?' Kim asked. 'Why did Owen leave?'

'Got thrown out for fighting.' Bert shook his head. 'I know it sounds bad, but my son wasn't a violent man. He was the kind of guy who wouldn't back down. Maybe that's my fault. I always taught him to stand up for himself.' Bert paused. 'You see, Owen got picked on when he was a kid. He was late to grow. When he finally sprouted up, he got tall. Big, too. He never forgot those kids who gave him a hard time.'

I was thinking about the hill behind Hailey's home. Kim had pointed out that Hailey could have been knocked out and carried up there. That would have taken someone with strength. Someone like Owen.

'Bert,' I began, carefully. 'We have to ask about Hailey. You're saying she and Owen weren't close?'

'They went out a couple of times. Had coffee. Dinner. Went to an exhibition at the art centre. Owen wanted it to be more. I'm sure he did. He was lonely, my boy.' He looked wistfully into the distance. 'Hailey wasn't interested, though. It hurt Owen. I know that. Heading off to those writing meetings must have been hard for him. But he didn't hurt her. Why would he?'

'So there was no animosity about anything?' I asked. 'Hailey was getting her novel published. There wasn't—'

Bert waved his hand. 'So you've heard about that,' he said.

I wasn't sure what he meant, so I simply nodded. 'Owen wasn't jealous,' Bert said. 'But the others were.'

'The other members of Plastic Apple?' Kim said, catching my eye.

'There was a fight at that last meeting,' Bert said, nodding. 'Everyone was upset about Hailey getting her book deal.'

We hadn't looked closely at Plastic Apple before. All the focus had been on Hailey and Owen. His history of violence had acted like a magnet, drawing everyone's attention from anything else. Could animosity from one of the other members have resulted in Hailey and Owen's deaths?

Bert continued. 'Not long after that meeting, Hailey's body was found in that ravine. The police took it as suicide—after all, she left a suicide note. It was her sister who kicked up a fuss. Said she'd been murdered, and Owen did it.'

I asked Bert if we could take a look at Owen's room. Unlike Rita, Bert had emptied his son's room. Bert took us out to the garage, the door opening upwards with a squeal. The place smelled of dust and motor oil. An old woodworking bench sat to one side. A fluorescent light fitting hung from the ceiling, casting a hard edge on piles of boxes in a corner.

Bert pointed to them. 'You can look through those,' he said, his gaze wistful. 'That's all I have of my boy.'

Without saying another word, he turned and staggered back inside.

'I feel sorry for him,' Kim said. 'Although Owen could be guilty.'

'It sounds like Owen liked to settle things with his fists.' I nodded to the boxes. 'Although these may tell us something different.'

We methodically went through the crates. Several contained Owen's clothing. There was little to discern from these other than Owen had been a sizeable man. Well-built and strong, which we had seen in photos.

It immediately became clear that Owen's obsession was with fantasy novels. He had hundreds of them. Sword and Sorcery books dominated, with several dating to Robert E Howard and other classic authors.

'Gosh,' she said. 'This reminds me of my cousin Brian. He loves those re-enactments of medieval warfare. Has his own suit of armour and sword. Goes off every Friday evening to fight.'

'I hear that's very popular.'

'Yes. You have to be careful, though. One of Brian's fingers got cut off with a replica sword.'

'My goodness,' I said. 'I assume the other guy did it by accident?'

'There was no other guy. Brian did it to himself.' Kim sighed. 'He's always been accident-prone.'

I searched Owen's papers. Besides documents from his old army and policing days, there were thousands of pages of handwritten stories and edits from his book.

'Good grief,' I whistled. 'There's a huge amount of paperwork here, and these are just notes. Owen must have been working on this for years. It could be several books.'

'Is there a copy of the actual book? Or books?'

'Completed versions? Not that I can see.'

'Is his writing any good?'

'It's hard to say.' I skimmed through a few pages. 'I think one of the books was called *The Cry of Kaled's Sword.* Seems solid. Looks like he knows how to write a sentence. Mind you, I have no idea how successful this would have been if it ever saw publication.' I continued through the wads of paper. Jammed in amongst them was a slim folder stuffed with pages. I was about to put it aside when I spotted a blank yellow envelope.

I peered inside. It contained two letters. I examined one while Kim took the other. 'This is interesting,' I said. 'It's from a publisher. They're interested in Owen's books and wanted to arrange a meeting with him.' I checked the date. 'Owen received this only a few days before his death, and it's from the same publisher that was releasing Hailey's book—Lancelot Press.'

Kim hadn't spoken. 'Look at this.'

The letter she held was typed and had only five words:

Stop or you'll regret it.

'What does it mean?' Kim asked. 'Stop—what? What was Owen doing that brought this on? This is similar to Hailey's note.'

'I have no idea.' I glanced back at the letter in my hand. 'Bert didn't mention that Owen had an interested publisher.'

'Let's ask him about it.'

'Sure.' I hesitated. 'But let's not mention the anonymous letter. Not yet. He's been through enough trauma regarding his son. He doesn't need us adding to it by inferring Owen was murdered and the police missed a clue.'

We returned to the living room, where we found the old man staring listlessly out the window. 'Owen didn't mention it to me,' Bert said when we asked him about the publisher.

'Although that's not surprising. I can't claim to know anything about books. The last one I read was in school.'

'Any chance we could take a look at Owen's completed novels?' Kim asked. 'There's a lot of pages in those boxes, though they seem to be notes and edits rather than complete books. Is his computer around?'

'Owen didn't use a computer. He wrote by hand. His books weren't in any of the boxes?'

'No,' I said. A novel could have been sent to the publisher, although publishers were specific in what they wanted from writers. Handwritten manuscripts were not the norm by any token. 'I understand you thought your house was broken into after Owen's disappearance.'

'I didn't notice at first. A few weeks later, I saw something in a drawer out of place.'

'Any idea how someone would have gotten in?'

He raised an eyebrow. 'This place isn't Fort Knox,' he said. 'I've never locked the doors because there's nothing to steal.'

We didn't have any further questions, so I thanked Bert and told him we'd be in touch.

He nodded. 'I want to know what happened to my son,' he said. 'I know he's dead. He must be. I just think it's a shame he didn't achieve much while he was here. Would have been nice if he'd made a success out of writing. Then, maybe, his life would have meant something.'

Telling Bert we'd stay in touch, we returned to my jeep. I slipped Trixie a doggy snack as we stood beside my vehicle. It was almost lunchtime, and I was feeling famished. And I'd had only one coffee. It was amazing I could still function with so little caffeine in my system!

Kim stroked her chin thoughtfully. 'So Hailey had a book that Lancelot Press was publishing,' she said. 'And Owen had interest from the same publisher. And, like Hailey, received a threatening letter.'

'Although Bert seemed to know nothing about it.'

'Bert didn't seem to know much about his son,' Kim said, sighing. 'It sounds like they didn't have a lot in common.'

'That happens sometimes.'

'I wonder what happened to Owen's books.'

'I don't know, but we'll have a better chance of working it out over a meal at Sandy's.'

Minutes later, we were huddled over burgers, chips, and coffee. I bit thoughtfully into a chip as we stared out at the ocean from the diner's front window. Although we hadn't learned much, I felt we'd made some headway.

'We have no idea what the other group members were like,' Kim said. 'According to Bert, the last meeting of Plastic Apple went into meltdown.'

'Although the meetings were usually helpful.'

Kim stared into space. 'But you can imagine what it would

be like,' she said. 'They're all working together until one of them finally makes a breakthrough. A *big* breakthrough. At first, they're excited, but then the resentment kicks in.'

'And Hailey's age wouldn't have helped either,' I added. 'Rita said Hailey was the youngest member of the group.'

Kim glanced at her watch. 'I've got to get into work this afternoon,' she said. 'I can only be away for so long before they think I've skipped the country. What will you be doing?'

'Another afternoon at ASFA,' I said, sighing. 'Although I don't know how.' I'd told Kim about knocking over the model of Laniakea. 'How can they still want me there when I've destroyed the universe?'

'They must be *very* forgiving.'

'Desperate more like it if I'm their idea of a celebrity.'

'What's happening over the next few days?'

'There's an excursion tomorrow to the Blackwood National Park. Apparently, a spaceship crashed and someone got taken by aliens near there.'

'Fantastic.' Kim looked entirely too cheerful. 'I'll come to that.'

I glanced at my phone. 'I better get going, or I'll be late.'

'What session's on this afternoon?'

'Oh, dear.' I read the agenda on my phone. 'It's called Alien Interactions and Abductions: Have You Been Probed?'

Kim stifled a grin. 'Bummer.'

7

'Please tell me there are leftovers,' I said as I plonked my bag down on the kitchen table.

Nan was in the kitchen, her head buried in the recesses of the freezer. 'There's some lentil and vegetable soup from last summer,' she said.

'Perfect.' Anything would be better than having to cook. I took the container from Nan, tipped it into a bowl, and nuked it in the microwave. Once it was ready, Nan and I settled down to eat and relax. 'How are the sewing ladies?'

'Sew-sew,' Nan said, giving me a weary smile. 'They're testing, though. All those old girls are a handful. They're voting on a new board, and this year no one standing for the role of president is under the age of eighty.'

'It's not like you to be ageist,' I said, swallowing a mouthful of soup. 'You're eighty-three and still a spring chicken.'

'Not everyone's as sprightly as me. One woman thinks John Cain is still the Victorian Premier.' She paused. 'Mind you, the ladies have asked me to stand.'

I looked at her with new respect. 'Wow,' I said. 'Will you accept?'

'I'm not sure. I'm busy with so many things that I need to watch what I do with my time. I also have a boyfriend to keep happy.'

'Men,' I said, smiling. 'Constant maintenance.'

After clearing the table and stacking the dishwasher, I took Trixie for a walk. We headed toward Cut Rock. It was a beautiful evening as I wandered along the bush track towards the coast. We were soon at the lookout and peering at the sea. A gentle zephyr wafted over the water, and I inhaled deeply.

Trixie let out a single bark.

'Hey you,' Todd Parker called.

I turned. The police sergeant wore jeans, a tight-fitting t-shirt, and a jacket. He had his three-legged greyhound Rocko with him and his friend Yvonne. She was a pretty brunette with short hair. We'd chatted a few times, and I liked her a lot. It was a shame she was living with Todd. He'd said they weren't a couple, but I couldn't help but wonder what went on behind closed doors.

'What brings you up here?' Yvonne asked.

I shrugged. 'All work and no play...'

'Todd tells me you're at the UFO conference. How are the aliens?'

'Do you mean the aliens or the conference attendees?' I asked. 'It's hard to tell one from the other.'

They laughed.

'Don't be too dismissive of flying saucers,' Todd said. 'We get reports about them all the time.'

'Really?'

'Every couple of months, people call us about lights in the Blackwood National Park.'

'Gosh. We're going out there tomorrow.' I told them about the supposed alien abduction. 'People ring you about lights?'

Todd shrugged. 'It's not illegal for people to visit the park at night,' he said. 'Anyone can go there. And monitoring the park is the work of park rangers, not the police. Still, people have seen activity.'

'What do you think is going on?'

'No idea. Several farms adjoin the park. It's probably nothing.'

I nodded. Heading to the national park was something I usually enjoyed. The national parks in Victoria were some of the wildest and most beautiful places in the world. Going there with a bunch of kooky flying saucer people wasn't something I was looking forward to.

Wishing me goodnight, Todd and Yvonne headed down the hill with Rocko. In the growing dusk, I made my way thoughtfully back to the house.

That night, I tossed and turned in bed, waking up several times with Todd and Yvonne in my thoughts. I kept on thinking of them together in his home. I finally counted sheep and eventually drifted off into a dreamless sleep.

The following day, I headed into the office and gave Harry a quick rundown of what had been happening at the UFO conference. He nodded, saying he hoped I was getting plenty of pictures.

'Pictures of what?' I asked, deadpan. 'People are sitting at a conference desk, and people are listening. It's not compelling viewing.'

'Well, you know what I always say. Pictures, pictures—'

'Yes, I know.' I hadn't forgiven him for sending me off on this crackpot assignment. 'I'll get a few photos. Actually, come to think of it, we're heading off to the national park this afternoon. Might get interesting shots there: a tree, a fern, maybe even a rock.'

'Don't be a smarty pants. We've all got to make the most of our assignments. Jay's doing a wonderful job with the Fabric and Sewing Association.'

'I'm sure he is,' I grumbled. 'By the way, I destroyed the universe on Tuesday.'

'Really? I hadn't noticed.'

I reluctantly told him about destroying the model that had taken them a year to make. By the time I finished, Harry was laughing so hard that tears ran down his cheeks.

'It's not funny!' I protested. 'One of the people who made it thought I was a CIA agent.'

'We know that could never be true,' Harry said, straight-faced. 'They're quite choosy about who they employ.'

Still grumbling, I went to my desk and typed up my notes. Jay came in, and I asked him about the conference.

'It's a bit hard to take,' he said. 'I can't tell one stitch from another. And they're so serious about everything.'

'Sewing is serious business.'

'But they're *really* serious. A competing organisation wants to merge with them: the Fabric Association of Australia. They both have about the same number of members. Half of the AFSA is keen to approve the merger. The other half are against it. I'm surprised there hasn't been a riot.'

I tried to imagine a bunch of old ladies starting a riot and couldn't. 'Well,' I said. 'At least it's a learning experience for you.'

'What are you up to today? More flying saucers?'

'That's this afternoon. Now I've got a meeting with Peter Wilson—and I'm not looking forward to it.'

Heading out of the office with Trixie, I drove to the library and picked Kim up. She climbed into the car with a sigh of relief. 'You've saved me from a fate worse than death,' she said. 'I'm currently cataloguing leaflets, and they are *terribly* time-consuming.'

I laughed. 'Life wasn't meant to be easy.'

'Are you looking forward to this meeting?'

'*Looking forward* are not quite the words I'd use,' I said. '*Dreading* is probably more appropriate.'

'He was never very cooperative.'

'Never cooperative?' I said. 'He issued no fewer than three defect notices to my jeep.'

'Wasn't one for the side mirror?'

'You can drive without one,' I informed Kim. 'But he had a personal grudge against us. It's almost like he didn't want our help.'

Kim raised an eyebrow. 'I wonder why that would be.'

'I don't know,' I grumbled. 'He should have been grateful.'

Smiling, Kim didn't speak again as we headed out of town past the lighthouse and onto Millicent Drive. We continued past the turnoff to Port Logan and Cullen Beach and on to Briar Lake, a scattered community living a kilometre inland from the ocean. A road led from the coast through thick bushland and over a bridge to the lake. Around this were a single general store and shacks nestled among the trees. It was impossible to tell where the border of one property ended and the next began.

Trixie, in the back seat, panted happily as she looked out the window. She liked visiting new places and loved the bush.

The lake was ideal for fishing, although the whole area was so off the beaten path it rarely got visitors.

Part of the problem was the lack of accommodation. There were few rental properties. I'd been here a few times over the years, and it was part hillbilly and part hippy community.

'It's hard to believe that Peter Wilson lives here,' Kim said. 'He was always so conservative.'

'It's hard to believe *anyone* lives here,' I said. Briar Lake was good for a holiday. It was ideal for fishing and thinking about life. The only problem was that after you did that for a while, there was literally nothing else to do. The general store was the only shop for miles around, and there were no other facilities. The beach wasn't far away, but you could only go there so often.

We drove on the dirt road around the lake, keeping an eye on letterboxes until we finally found Peter Wilson's place.

It was similar to the other homes, a weatherboard building nestled among some swamp oaks with a tiny jetty jutting into the water. Stopping the car, we got out as a side door of the building clattered open, and an overweight figure appeared. The ex-sergeant wore a flannelette shirt, faded jeans, and an expression somewhere between amusement and resignation.

'Well, well, well,' Peter Wilson said. 'If it isn't Holmes and Watson. And Trixie the wonder dog.'

At least he hadn't shot us. That was a positive start. 'Peter,'

I said. 'How have you been?'

'Relaxed. Glad to be away from it all.' He nodded to the cabin. 'Come on in. I've just made a pot of coffee.'

The interior was timber, pine by the look of it. There seemed to be only three rooms. The main kitchen/dining area, a bedroom, and a bathroom. Although it would have been tiny for a family, it probably suited a single, retired man. Pots and pans hung from a rack over a stone-clad bench in the kitchen. A rocky fireplace nestled in one corner and a rocking chair in another, a small bookcase of dogeared books beside it.

The place had a television, but it was the smallest I'd seen in a long time; obviously, Peter Wilson wasn't too interested in watching TV. As much as I hated to admit it, the cabin had a cozy feel. Living here probably suited the ex-cop to a T.

We gathered around a kitchen table where he poured us coffee. He even had a bowl where Trixie could drink water.

'Used to have a dog,' he said. 'You might remember him: Benny. He died.'

'Sorry to hear that,' Kim said.

'He was old. That's how things go.' Peter settled down opposite. 'Todd told me you girls are looking into Hailey Lawrence's death. I thought that was settled.'

I hesitated. 'Questions have been raised,' I said. 'Rita Lawrence approached me. She doesn't believe Hailey's death was suicide.'

'Nothing new about that. She always thought someone murdered Hailey. Owen Stamett was her top suspect. So what's changed?'

I felt defensive but tried not to show it. 'Nothing,' I said, 'I suppose. But Rita's after a definitive answer on what happened to her sister. If Hailey killed herself, then so be it. But if Owen killed her, then he got away scott-free.'

Peter stroked his chin. 'If Owen disappeared, then he made a good job of it. His phone last bounced off a cell tower near Elk's Gap. Todd told me there's been no movement on his accounts.'

'And his father's never heard from him,' Kim added. 'It's one thing to disappear. It's another to abandon your father and friends.'

'If Hailey were murdered, then Owen was the likely suspect. It does fit. I'll admit that.' He paused. 'I always felt there was more to that case than met the eye. And I know what you're thinking. That I didn't support you when you came asking about Hailey and Owen. What you could never accept was that anyone can have conjecture. Anyone can gossip or put forward theories or ideas. That's easy. It's a different thing entirely to investigate the case, track down the guilty party and prove it in court.' He leaned forward. 'You know, I had lots of cases go wrong at the last moment. The judge threw them out because of a lack of evidence. Or the jury gave the benefit of the doubt to the guilty person.'

'But what if they were innocent?' I asked.

'Sure. *But what if they were guilty?*' Peter's face hardened. 'And there were a bunch of people I saw leaving the court-room, sneering at me. Sneering at the judge. Sneering at the victim's families.' He stopped. 'But none of that answers your questions. All right. I thought the whole thing seemed fishy. You know Hailey and Owen belonged to a writing group?'

I nodded.

'The truth is I always thought there were a lot of secrets in that group. There was bad blood among them. Or, at least, that's the impression I got. They pretended to be buddies. Beneath the surface, it was a whole different story.'

'You didn't follow up at the time?' Kim asked.

The ex-cop shook his head. 'I would have—if I'd had a team of detectives and constables. But I didn't. We had half a dozen cops at Cape Carson who had to cover the whole region. There's only so much a team that size can handle.'

'Well,' I said evenly. 'Kim and I will follow up with the writing group.'

'They used to meet at the bookshop. You know the one?'

'Unicorn Books?'

'That's it. Ian Westlok owns it. A nice bloke. Bit lonely, though. His wife up and left him four years back. Ran off with some guy to Queensland. He's not been the same since.'

I knew Ian, having been into his shop dozens of times over the years.

Unicorn Books was a local institution with the enviable reputation of never closing. It opened every day of the year, including Christmas and New Year's Day. The shop had been running for half a century and sold new and used books in addition to DVDs.

'Start with him,' Peter suggested. 'He can give you an insight into the group. They met there for years.'

This sounded like a dismissal, and Peter Wilson stood up to confirm it. He followed us outside to where my jeep was parked. 'You've still got the same car?' he said, shaking his head. 'Boy. How many defects did I write up for that old thing?'

'Three.' I was defensive about my car. 'And my jeep's still running fine.'

'There's a difference between drivable and fit to be driven.' Peter flashed a rare grin. 'Good luck with the case, girls. Hope you discover more than me. Maybe something happened to Hailey and Owen, but I have no idea what.'

8

'And this is where it occurred,' Barry Rycroft told the group. 'The incident known as the Blackwood Encounter.'

We were at the edge of the Blackwood National Park. It was mid-afternoon, and a surprising number of people had joined us. Around fifty members of AFSA were assembled in the clearing, including Jasper and Neo. Although some wore t-shirts adorned with flying saucers, most looked more like they were on an excursion to the country. It was a refreshing change from being stuck in the hotel.

Kim was with me, which was a relief. Although seeing as how interested she was in UFOs, I suspected that keeping her away would have been impossible.

The day was lovely.

Giant beech trees and ferns surrounded the clearing. Brightly coloured Eastern Rosellas went flitting across the tree tops. A sulphur-crested cockatoo screamed raucously from a nearby branch. I inhaled the scent of eucalyptus and lush undergrowth. It was intoxicating.

Nothing's as good as the Australian bush, I thought.

'It happened back in 1997,' Barry continued. 'A scout group was camping in this area. They were on a three-day hike from Delltown to the coast. It's rugged forest all the way. Although a fit adult can walk it in two days, this wasn't a race. The scout-masters were teaching the kids survival skills and achieving points for their Duke of Edinburgh awards.

'They camped in this clearing, intending to stay overnight and leave early the next morning. It's only a few hours' walk to the coast from here. As they had the previous night, they'd made camp, cooked dinner, and told ghost stories.' Barry's gaze moved across the group. 'Maybe some of you are thinking they were impressionable kids and that they cooked up the story in their heads. That they imagined everything that was to happen. Don't forget there were three adults with them. Two scout masters and a parent. They saw what happened later too.'

It was quiet in the clearing. Even the cockatoo had fallen to silence.

'Everyone went to bed early. And don't forget, this was the second night of camping. They'd stayed up late the first night, but the kids were tired now. So were the adults. Maybe every-one was looking forward to it being finished.' He paused. 'You can imagine how peaceful it is at night. Besides the odd owl and the foraging of a possum or wombat, it's dead silent, like the inside of a cave.

'Around three o'clock, when everyone was asleep, there was the sound of an explosion that shook the forest. Everyone woke up. One of the scoutmasters later said he thought the world had come to an end, the ground shook so hard. People were up and about with torches, although it was clear where the sound had come from. The smell of burnt timber was in the air, and a glow was coming from the west.' Barry pointed. 'It was over there where the object crashed.'

Everyone's gaze moved towards a wall of trees.

'One of the scoutmasters decided to follow a trail into the bush,' Barry said. 'He told the others to stay behind. Of course, no one listened. Not the adults. Not even the kids. It was obvious something weird had happened, and everyone wanted to know what.

'They followed him down the path and arrived in a newly burnt-out area. It was vast. A hundred feet across. Trees had been destroyed, pulverised by the blast. In the heart of the mess was an impact hole. Something had crashed from the sky and hit the ground hard. There were even the remains of some creatures. There was blood.' He paused dramatically. 'And it wasn't red.'

Good grief! I thought. *Is anyone really believing this hog-wash?*

I glanced around.

Much to my dismay, Kim seemed transfixed by the story. So did many others, although some looked a little bored. I wondered if they'd heard it before.

'One of the strangest things about the crash site was the light. Everyone agreed later that everything had an orange glow. The scouts ran around and put out spot fires.

'Fortunately, the forest was lush and green, and this hike was in the wet season. Things would have been different at the height of summer. It was while they were doing this that they found the wreckage.' Barry studied the crowd. 'AFSA is lucky to have one of the only remaining pieces. No doubt you've heard us talk about it. Yes, I've brought along the famed Blackwood Relic.'

A collective *oooh* went up around the crowd.

Barry's backpack had been sitting at his feet. Now he picked it up and pulled out a shining piece of silver metal. While other people looked impressed, my own response was a little more blasé. I thought it looked more like a tailpipe off someone's car than wreckage from a flying saucer.

'It's too valuable to hand around,' Barry explained. 'But I'm allowing a viewing later in the week at the session on alien technology.' He handled the piece like an ancient Sumerian tablet. 'Government agents would love to get their hands on this. We can never be too careful.'

Neo sidled over. 'Spies are everywhere,' she whispered.

'Yep,' I sighed. 'It's a problem.'

'We're going to take a walk around to the crash site,' Barry continued. 'Everyone please stick together—and be careful. It's possible that something is still out here. Raise your hand if you feel dizzy or experience time dilation.'

'Time dilation?' I said to Neo.

'Time passing very fast,' she said. 'Or slowly.'

I nodded.

Time is going slowly, I thought. *I think it's boredom.*

Still, there was a good opportunity for a photo here. Before Barry could put the tailpipe, or whatever it was away, I arrowed over. 'Mind if I take a look?' I asked.

'I'm afraid not.' Barry frowned. 'If I let you handle it, then I've got to let everyone.'

'A picture, then?'

Barry nodded reluctantly. He took the object out, and I snapped a photo. After returning it to the bag, Barry drew near. 'I'd rather that picture didn't see publication,' he said quietly. 'It could be worth my life if certain agencies knew I had this in my possession.'

'Okay.' I was sure I wanted to use the picture in the paper, although now wasn't the time to discuss it. 'Thanks for the talk.'

He nodded. Everyone had started toward the crash site, and

Barry joined them.

Kim drew close. 'Do you think that's really part of a space-ship?' she whispered.

'No!' I said, possibly too loudly, as a couple of people glanced around. I lowered my voice. 'It's a piece of junk. It could be anything!'

'So how did it end up out here?'

I sighed. 'We don't have any evidence that this is true. Every-thing he told us could be baloney.'

'Maybe. Or that thing could have come from...' She nodded skyward. 'We could already be infested with alien microbes and end up as blobs.'

'I already am a blob. It's from eating too many burgers.'

We trailed after the group into another clearing.

This was roughly circular, crowded with knee-high ferns, and surrounded by blackwood trees. There was no sign of any fire, and no trees destroyed in a crash. It was more like a picnic ground.

Although this was a lovely day in the forest, I thought this was otherwise a complete waste of time. Much to my dismay, some people were at the edges of the clearing, searching the undergrowth.

'Should we join the search?' Kim asked.

'Kim,' I said. 'You're my best friend, but I'm disowning you if you join those people.'

'You're no fun, Rosie.'

'You'll be thanking me if someone catches an alien disease.'

Barry strode to the centre of the clearing and raised his voice. 'Okay, everyone,' he said. 'We'll continue to the house where the Berman family disappeared.'

We traipsed after him and soon arrived at a narrow tarred road running alongside the national park. On the other side of the road sat a derelict building surrounded by overgrown fields. An old weatherboard place, it had clearly seen better days. The roof was rusting, and part of it had caved in. There were holes in the walls, and several windows were missing. A storm metal fence surrounded the place, emblazoned with a red and white *Danger Do Not Enter* sign.

Once the group had gathered, Barry pointed dramatically at the house. 'A week passed before anyone realised what had happened to the Berman family,' he said. 'There were four of them: mum, dad, and their two kids. The alarm was only raised when an elderly aunt dropped by and found the house empty. Their car was still in the driveway, and the rooms full of belongings. But they were gone. It was as if they'd disappeared off the face of the Earth.' He paused dramatically and nodded to the skies. 'And I believe they did.'

Neo sidled up. 'They were taken,' she said. 'Probably stuck in a zoo. What do you think, Rosie?'

'Oh yes,' I said, vaguely agreeing that a family may have had been kidnapped from regional Victoria and was now residing in a zoo on the Bladeblah home world. 'Anything's possible.'

While people *oohed* and *aahed* at the derelict building, Jasper and Barry had moved to the edge of the road. There seemed to be a disagreement in progress.

Jasper raised his voice. '...relic belongs to the Association!' he was saying. 'Others must be allowed to see it.'

'They can see it whenever they want,' Barry replied. 'But someone has to be its keeper. You know there's a market for relics. They're priceless.'

My journalistic instinct kicked in. 'Priceless?' I said, as I hurried over with Kim and Neo. 'You mean people pay money for pieces of...uh, alien spaceships?'

'Lots of money,' Barry informed us. 'A piece in the US sold recently for a million dollars.'

A million dollars! I thought about the lump of junk Barry was toting about in his backpack. *And the thing looks like it fell off a car!*

'Everyone will be getting a closer look at the relic when I give my metallurgical talk later,' Barry said.

'The relic should be accessible to all the members,' Jasper insisted.

'After all,' Neo added, 'we *all* paid for it.'

I was dying to ask how much the AFSA had paid but now wasn't the time.

'I'm the President of AFSA,' Barry said firmly. 'And I'm the keeper of the relic. The final decision lies with me.'

And with this, he stalked off to speak to the other attendees, leaving Jasper and Neo to wearily shake their heads.

'Something's got to be done about him,' Jasper muttered.

'Jasper?' I said. 'What do you mean?'

Neo spoke up. 'Barry's been president for twenty years,' she said. 'He's done a fantastic job, but we need new leadership.' She turned to Jasper. 'That could be you. You've been treasurer for all that time. You need to step up.'

'I don't know.' Jasper shook his head. 'People have Barry on a pedestal. He started AFSA, he's been the driving force, and turned us into the organisation we are.'

'It's time for a change,' Neo insisted.

Kim and I exchanged glances.

All is not well in the world of flying saucers!

9

'So this is where Owen disappeared,' Kim said.

It was early morning, and we had arrived at Elk's Gap. The spot was a narrow valley several kilometres from the coast. It was a beautiful place, wild and remote, with high sloping hills crowded with thick bush. Trees and low-lying ferns pushed to the edge of the road. With some difficulty, Kim and I had found a small clearing to pull into. We climbed from my jeep, and I slipped Trixie a homemade doggy snack.

'Owen Stamett didn't actually disappear here,' I reminded her. 'This was the last known connection from his mobile. The signal pinged off towers in this area.'

'So what happened?'

That was the sixty-four dollar question. 'Assuming Owen vanished voluntarily, he turned the phone off or removed the SIM card and ditched the phone somewhere in the under-growth.' I nodded to the bush. 'You can see why it was never recovered.'

At the best of times, the Australian bush was a mishmash of ferns, fallen logs, vines, and trees. Anything that went in was swallowed whole by the undergrowth. Finding something as tiny as a phone was impossible.

'His car's never been found, which means he kept driving,' Kim added, thoughtfully. 'He then discarded the vehicle and swapped it for another. This road continues onto the highway. From there, you can go anywhere: Melbourne, South Australia, the world.'

This all made sense if Owen murdered Hailey. It fit the story of an obsessive man who killed the target of his affection before disappearing. It had been done before. Even in this era of digital tracking, a determined person could still create another identity and vanish into the ether.

'That makes sense,' I said, 'except his credit cards and bank account have never been used. He's never been sighted. Owen somehow dropped off the grid and was never seen again.'

'That indicated a lot of organisation,' Kim said.

'And connections. It's not that easy to disappear. It takes money and time to set it up.' Years ago, Sergeant Wilson had confirmed that there'd been no large withdrawals from Owen's bank account before or after his disappearance. 'It's hard enough to vanish *with* money, let alone without it.'

'Which takes us back to the idea that he killed himself.'

I peered into the bush. Never mind discarding a mobile

phone out here. A person could wander into the undergrowth, take their own life, and never be seen again. Locating their body would be impossible.

'Which seems to make more sense,' I said, 'except there's no sign of his car.'

'Someone else could have brought him here and left with it,' Kim said, frowning. 'That would mean he had an accomplice.'

'No one else's name has ever come up in connection to Owen's disappearance. The police investigated all his known associates.'

Kim bit her lip. 'Is there a landmark around here?' she said. 'Something that would have significance to someone?' She pointed. 'What about up there?'

I followed her gaze to a hilly clifftop. 'You're thinking he could have followed the same plan as Hailey?' I said. 'That would make sense. It doesn't explain what happened to his car, but it bears looking into.'

Examining the map on my phone, I discovered a single side road headed from here to a spot named Jeffkins Lookout. We got back in my jeep and took the turnoff.

Trixie barked as my jeep jolted about on the way up. 'It's fine, girl,' I said.

'You can fool Trixie with that,' Kim said, swaying from side to side. 'But not me.'

'It's just a bit uneven.'

The jeep hit a nasty pothole, and we lurched to the right. 'Okay,' I amended. 'It's not a great road.'

We soon reached the lookout and got out. There was a retaining fence, so we leaned over the side. The drop was about a hundred metres.

'You wouldn't survive a fall from here,' I said, shaking my head.

'Your hiking days would be over,' Kim agreed.

We peered out across the valley. There was little to see. As lookouts went, this one wouldn't be making it into Australia's top ten tourist destinations any time soon. The Australian bush was beautiful, but it was also wild. To the untrained observer, it could appear to be a screen of unending sameness. Only on closer inspection could an observer make out a myriad of detail: individual ferns, the curling branches of primeval trees, and ancient rocks dotted with aquamarine moss.

I focused. 'What's that?' I asked.

Kim followed my gaze. Mingling among the greenery was a tiny splash of red.

'A flower?' she suggested.

'Maybe. But it's the only one.'

She stared critically at the patch. 'You're not suggesting we tramp down there? That's rugged terrain. We'd never find it.'

'I don't know about *never*,' I said cautiously.

But I could see Kim's point. There didn't appear to be

a track through there. It looked like thick, undulating bush all the way from the road. Traipsing through it was virtually impossible. Although I'd done a fair bit of bushwalking in my younger days, that was a long time back and not through anything that dense.

I wasn't sure what to do.

'Let's head down to the road,' Kim suggested. 'Maybe there's a fire trail that leads to the base of the cliff, and it's not visible through the trees.'

We climbed back into my jeep and drove back down. After reaching the main road, we went along it slowly, peering into the thick bush for routes not shown on the map. It turned out to be a fruitless search. There were either no fire trails, or they were so overgrown as to be impassable.

As we pulled over to the side, Kim's phone rang. She flashed me a smile as she answered. 'Hey, Adrian. What's up?' They chatted for a moment. 'Here's an idea. How about that dinner party we've been talking about.' She listened. 'Yeah, Rosie and a few others...wonderful...good...I'll work out the details with her.'

She hung up. 'You heard all that?' she said. 'You and Todd will be an item before you know it.'

'I don't know. I think Todd's firmly ensconced with Yvonne.'

Kim hit my arm. 'They're friends!' she said. 'How many

times do you need to be told?'

'Lots of times! I can't get those terrible images out of my head!'

'You're a crazy woman! Tell Todd the dinner party's on! That's an order!'

Before I could respond, my phone rang, and I answered: Rita Lawrence.

'I'm wondering how you're going with the investigation,' were her first words.

I gave her a quick rundown of what we'd discovered. As I spoke, I felt like I was relating a story she already knew. We'd asked a lot of questions and not learnt a lot. Not unless you included some threatening notes and a flash of red at the bottom of the cliff that could be a body or a piece of junk.

She listened in silence until I'd finished. 'You're right about Plastic Apple,' she said. 'Hailey had a love-hate relationship with the group. She told me there was a huge fight at that last meeting. It was a shame because the group had been helpful.'

'We'll speak to the members,' I promised.

'And visit the bookshop, too,' Rita added. 'Ian, the owner, is lovely and knew all of them well.'

Thanking her, I hung up and turned to Kim. 'We're off to bookshop.'

Kim beamed. 'Great,' she said. 'That's my kind of place.'

10

I took a deep breath. 'Ah,' I said. 'One of my favourite places in Cape Carson.'

'There's nothing so good as the smell of books,' Kim replied.

'Except maybe fresh air...and freshly baked cookies...and flowers...'

'That's debatable.'

We were at Unicorn Books. The place was one of the oldest buildings in Cape Carson, a Georgian-style place that dated to the early days of the town.

Constructed from Harcourt granite, the bookshop was originally built as a grand old home for the Tillbury family. They were British migrants who moved to Australia in the 1800s to grow crops and herd sheep. As it turned out, they did well for themselves and built their grand old house on what was now Third Avenue, a few blocks back from the beach.

After the last of the Tillburys had died out, the place had

passed from one family to another until it fell into ruin. Back in the nineteen seventies, an enterprising merchant had turned it into a used goods warehouse. This had gradually morphed into a used bookstore that became Unicorn Books. It now housed over fifty thousand books, mostly used but some new, and a selection of second-hand DVDs.

Opposite the entrance was the front desk where Ian Westlok sat. In addition to a herd of part-time bookshop workers, part of the shop was a dedicated café. Books were coming and going all the time, as well as supplies for the cafe. Ian mostly managed the place alone; I don't know how he did it. A sign hung over the counter: *We Never Close.*

Forty years old, he was a big giant of a man, rotund with fat fingers and wore black, round spectacles. He was constantly smiling and joking and one of the most cheerful people I'd ever met. His face broke into an easy grin when he saw us.

'Rosie!' he said. 'And Kim!' He held up his hands. 'Don't tell me! You're after mystery novels! Agatha Christie! Dorothy L Sayers! Conan Doyle!'

We laughed.

'Afraid not,' I said. 'Actually, we're after some information.'

'Ah,' Ian said, nodding. 'This is an official visit. A mystery you're investigating?'

'It's about Hailey Lawrence.'

Ian frowned. 'Hailey...Hailey...where do I know that name?

Oh goodness. I remember her. She was a member of the Plastic Apple writing group.' He shook his head sadly. 'Terrible what happened to her. So terrible.'

'Can we chat for a moment?' Kim asked.

Fortunately, Ian had an assistant who could look after the counter while we crowded into his office. The room was a tiny chamber, made even smaller by the boxes of books jamming the corners and the piles stacked high on Ian's desk. He settled snugly into his seat before giving Trixie a pat. 'Good thing you don't own a Saint Bernard,' he said. 'There's no way we'd all fit in here. Now, you were asking about Hailey Lawrence.'

'And the Plastic Apple group,' I said. 'They met here for some time?'

Ian nodded. 'Oh yes,' he said. 'Years and years. It's a shame they stopped. The club ran for decades. They met in our cellar. It's not big. Was a storeroom back when the Tillburys lived here. Now it holds our science collection.' He added, 'Sadly, not our biggest movers.'

'What do you remember of Hailey?' Kim asked.

'Not a whole lot, to be honest.' He stroked his chin. 'Let's see. The last time I saw her was at that final meeting three years ago. Around the time of the earthquake.'

'The April Fool's Day quake?' I said.

We didn't get many earthquakes on this part of the coast, although the odd one did shake the shelves and rattle the animals. The one on April Fool's Day three years before had been a 5.9 on the Richter scale and had caused minor damage throughout the area.

'I seem to recall the usual crowd turning up,' Ian continued. 'There was Jacob. He organised the room bookings. Was part of the club since forever. Then there was Asher. He's worked at the council for years. Belonged to the club a long time, too. I got the impression that Plastic Apple was more of a social club for him than anything else.'

'And the other members?'

'Well,' Ian considered, 'there's Bella. Not the most pleasant woman. Owned a rather nasty dog.' Ian smiled at Trixie. 'Not like you, girl. Okay, and then there was Kylie Crow. She writes romance novels. A few of her books come in every so often. They seem to sell. And Piper. Another young woman. Was friendly enough.'

'That was all?' Kim asked. 'That's not a big group.'

'The numbers fluctuated a lot over the years. That happens in every community group. I still see them all. They come in to buy books.' He rubbed his chin. 'I never had a lot to do with them. Just let them use the room. It was a shame the club closed. It had been running for decades.'

Kim spoke up. 'Owen was a member too,' she said.

'Oh, yes,' Ian said. 'That's true. I forgot him. Well, that fits in with that whole story about Hailey not killing herself and

Owen being responsible. Then, of course, he left town after that.'

'What do you think happened?' I asked.

Ian shrugged. 'It's hard to say,' he said. 'I remember Hailey. A nice young woman, although depressive. Sometimes downright melancholy.' He stopped. 'She did say something to me about Owen one time.'

I waited.

'She called Owen a stalker. Said he'd been harassing her for a date. I said she should complain to the police and she replied that he wasn't that bad. Just insistent and wouldn't take no for an answer.'

I nodded thoughtfully. 'Thanks. Kim and I might take a look around.'

'Of course.' Ian smiled. 'You've got to buy something, though. Some new Ellery Queens have arrived. They're quite old.'

Kim grumbled. 'You know us too well.'

'That's my job!' Ian laughed.

Leaving Ian in his office, Kim and I wandered around the store. It was impossible to not be enthralled by the selection of books. The place had an intoxicating feel. The walls were whitewashed timber with red cedar bookshelves stretching to the ceiling. There were over twenty rooms in the building. We didn't go into every room but instead headed for the cellar.

We descended a narrow timber staircase that was closed in on both sides until we reached the bottom. Here, it opened onto a small square room with timber joists running across the low ceiling.

This was where Plastic Apple had held its meetings.

Seven timber chairs surrounded a small coffee table. Lining the walls were shelves stuffed with hundreds of science and maths books. The place smelt of stonework and old paper.

And maybe even mould. A huge crack in one wall, now repaired, disappeared behind the timber shelving.

'I can see why Ian stuck the Plastic Apple members down here,' Kim said. 'It's not a fun place.'

I nodded. 'I don't remember ever coming down here,' I said. 'I rarely venture past the crime and mystery section.'

'Can we take a look in the cookbook room?' Kim asked.

'You're after recipes?'

'I'm trying to make an impression on my man.'

It was a delight to hear Kim speak in such a way. *My man.* What a lovely phrase. And how beautiful to see such a look on her face. It was like she was a teenager all over again. We headed back up to the cookery section on the ground floor. Twice the size of the tiny cellar, there was another table here, surrounded by four leather-backed chairs. The shelves lining the room were arranged into regions of cooking: India, Japan, South America, and so forth.

'What will we have?' Kim mused. 'Italian? Thai? Chinese?'

'You're in charge,' I said. 'And you know my stomach doesn't discriminate. But I thought Adrian was doing the cooking?'

'He'll appreciate my input.'

'I'm sure.'

As she trawled through cookbooks, I took out my phone and checked for messages. 'Good grief!' I yelled. 'I'm due back at the UFO conference!'

'You go,' Kim said. 'I'll stay here a while.'

Fifteen minutes later, I was hurrying into the conference room at the Kilkenny Arms. Although the room was filled with people, there were only two committee members at the front table: Neo and Jasper.

I grabbed a seat. 'Where's Barry?' I puffed.

'Not here,' Neo said. 'It's not like him to be late.'

At that moment, the door I'd raced through burst open, and Barry appeared looking pale and disoriented. He staggered into the room. 'The relic!' he said. 'It's been stolen!' His gaze focused on Jasper. 'And you're the one who took it!'

11

'Okay,' Todd said. 'Let me see if I've got this right.'

The last hour had been tumultuous after Barry's accusation. An argument had broken out between the two men that had escalated into a full-blown fight. Punches had been thrown, and the men had to be separated. This led to the police being called, the room cleared, and the session cancelled. The only people left here were the AFSA committee members, cops, and the manager Natalie Cook. She was an attractive stick-skinny woman with honey-blonde hair and an upturned nose.

Trixie seemed a little shaken after the fight. I patted her on the head. She disliked violence as much as me.

Todd continued. 'Barry went to his hotel room to retrieve this so-called piece of flying saucer for this afternoon's session.'

'There's no *so-called* about it,' Neo said. 'It's wreckage from a visitor's ship. Evidence that extra-terrestrials are visiting our world.'

'And you're...' Todd consulted his notes, '...Neo.'

'That's me.'

The big policeman looked like he wanted to say more but held his tongue. He turned back to Barry. 'And what did you find?' he asked.

'It had been searched,' Barry said. 'Turned upside-down. I kept the relic in one of my bags, and now it's been stolen.' He pointed to Jasper. 'By him!'

'I had nothing to do with the theft!' Jasper snapped. 'Why would I take it?'

'To sell it. The relic's worth a fortune.'

Todd cut in. 'How much?' he asked.

'A million dollars,' he said. 'Maybe more.'

'Right.' Todd gave me a sideways glance. 'A million dollars for…a piece of flying saucer.'

'It's priceless,' Neo added.

'Hmm.'

Natalie Cook cut in. 'There were some minor thefts a few years back,' she said. 'That's why we now have safes in all the rooms.'

'I couldn't trust one of those things,' Barry said.

'A likely explanation!' Jasper snapped. 'Confess Barry: you've stolen it to sell!'

Barry's face filled with fury as he stepped toward Jasper.

Neo leapt to her feet. 'No!' she said. 'We've been friends for years. Barry wouldn't do something like that.'

'Gentlemen,' I said. 'May I suggest a truce? We'll do some investigating and take it from there?'

Both men reluctantly nodded.

'Okay,' I said. 'Barry, maybe we could take a look at your hotel room.'

'Of course. We'll go there now.'

Jasper stood. 'Good,' he said. 'I'd like to view the scene of the crime for myself—'

'Not right now,' Todd interrupted smoothly. 'Stay here, please. Constable Turner will ask you a few more questions.'

We followed Barry to his room. It was on the hotel's top floor, the same level as where Neo, Jasper, and several other convention members were staying. As Barry had said, his bags had been upended and the clothing flung over the floor.

Todd glanced around. 'What did it look like? This...relic?'

'I'll show you,' Barry said, snatching up a picture from the floor. 'It's about a foot across and twice as long. Light as a feather. Obviously not of Earthly origin.'

'How do you know?'

'I had it tested years ago.' Barry sighed. 'The relic is made from an aluminium alloy. Ideal for space travel.'

'So you left it with the lab?'

'No. It never left my sight.'

'Because you're worried someone would steal it?'

'Not just that.' Barry looked sideways at us. 'Officer, I know you're an innocent pawn in all this, but government agencies wouldn't want the true nature of this item to be revealed. It's well known that governments have been conspiring for decades to hide the existence of visitors to our world. That's why a piece of wreckage like this is so valuable. It's definitive proof that aliens are visiting Earth. Weirdness abounds!'

Trixie and I exchanged glances.

Can't argue with that, I thought, slipping her a doggy snack.

I glanced back at the door. 'Barry,' I said. 'How would they have gotten in? That's a hefty lock on the door.'

Barry rolled his eyes. 'Anyone can pick a lock,' he said. 'There are instructions on the internet for doing so. Getting into the room would have been child's play. What you must do now is search Jasper's room before he can dispose of the relic—if he hasn't done so already.'

'You seem pretty convinced that Jasper took it,' I said. 'Why not anyone else?'

'Jasper's wanted to be AFSA president for years. Although he's a competent treasurer, Jasper's not an organiser. And he can't speak to the media. Whenever he's spoken to reporters, he's made us sound like a bunch of weirdos.'

We headed back downstairs and asked Jasper if we could search his room. He immediately agreed. 'It's no skin off my nose,' Jasper said, glaring at Barry. 'I have nothing to hide.'

Todd and I trooped after Jasper to his room, where he flung

the door open wide. 'There you are,' he said, clearly miffed. 'Search all you like.'

Sighing, Todd slipped on gloves and went through the room. He searched under the bed, in wardrobes, and Jasper's bags. Todd even opened up the tiny bar fridge near the sink. In the end, he nodded and returned to us.

'Nothing,' he said.

'Of course!' Jasper snapped. 'We all know what this is about.'

I exchanged glances with Todd. 'Okay,' I said. 'What is that exactly?'

'Control of the AFSA! Barry's been president for twenty years. People are sick of his leadership, particularly the way he has complete control of the relic. He's even dubbed himself *The Keeper of the Relic*! It never leaves his sight!' He lowered his voice. 'Several members have approached me recently, asking that I take the helm.'

'So you think the theft of the relic...' I began.

'Is a ploy to cast aspersions on me. If I were suspected of a crime—especially something as serious as this—then no one would want me as AFSA president.'

'Do you want to be president?'

Jasper hesitated. 'Not at first,' he said. 'But I've thought about it, and I think I would make a good president.' His face darkened. 'Although that's probably impossible now the relic is gone.'

We returned to the meeting room where Barry, Neo, and some of the other AFSA members had assembled.

Todd explained that a thorough search of Barry and Jasper's rooms had been conducted and nothing found.

He asked Barry to accompany him to the station.

'In the meantime,' he said to the others, 'please play nicely. We may be a long way from the big smoke, but we still arrest people for disturbing the peace.'

I headed out with Todd and Barry. They left in Todd's police car, leaving Trixie and me on the footpath.

It was mid-afternoon, and my stomach was growling.

I hadn't eaten since breakfast, and I was feeling seriously caffeine-deprived.

My phone rang. 'Harry?' I said.

'Rosie,' he replied. 'I hear there's been some excitement at the UFO conference.'

'That's one way of putting it.' I quickly explained what had happened. This was the day we went to print, and I hadn't filed a single story all week. 'Is there still some room in the paper?'

'For the theft of a UFO artifact? Are you kidding? But have you got pictures?'

'Absolutely.'

'Then give me 300 words.'

I raced back to the office with Trixie. Within minutes, I

had begun pounding out the story on my computer. Jay came stumbling in the door after a while.

'Oh, Rosie,' he groaned. 'I need help.'

'Huh?' I glanced up from my computer. 'What's up?'

'It's those ladies from AFSA.' He slumped at this desk. 'I'm sorry I ever agreed to help them. They've got me modelling outfits and posing for pictures at sewing machines. I feel like I'm being used.'

He pulled out his phone and showed me an image of him seated at a sewing machine, trying to thread the bobbin. The look on his face was utter confusion, as if he'd been told to fly a plane with no instruction. I burst out laughing.

'That should be on the front page,' I said.

'What?' Jay looked horrified. 'No!'

'It'll be great.' I raised my voice. 'Harry! Hold the front page! Jay's got a fantastic picture!'

'No...I...' Jay started.

Harry called back. 'Send it through, Jay!'

Grumbling, Jay sent the picture to Harry. This was followed by silence—and then a roar of laughter.

'Yes!' he yelled from his office. 'Front page it is!'

Jay glared at me. 'I hate you, Rosie Ryan.'

'We all have to make sacrifices for the greater good. I gave up a successful career as an entertainment reporter to tell stories about aliens and people in tinfoil hats.' I continued to type.

'And you know what Harry always says: pictures, pictures, pictures!'

I took another half hour to finish my story and send it to Harry. He was grateful for my piece on the UFO conference. Harry loved variety in the paper. After that, I headed down the road to Sandy's Diner.

Sandy was wiping down the counter as I entered. 'Hey Rosie,' she said. 'The usual?'

'Thanks. I'm on my last legs. Only a jumbo double-shot caramel latte can save me.'

'I'll make it quick. I don't want you dying on the premises. It's bad for business.'

Agreeing that having a dead body in your diner did nothing for trade, I headed to a nearby booth and settled in. I'd only been there a minute when my ex-husband George entered.

We'd been on frosty terms since his brother Nico was sent to jail. Unfortunately, I was partly the cause of his incarceration. I'd caught Nico involved in illegal activities, and he was now spending time behind bars.

George spotted me. He gave me a tight smile and ordered a takeaway coffee before arrowing over. 'Didn't expect to see you here,' he said.

Didn't expect to? I thought. *Or hoped you wouldn't?*

'How are things?' I asked.

'Okay. Getting on with life.'

I suppose that meant he was trying to put the past behind him. Maybe that included our falling out over Nico.

He paused, looking a little uncomfortable. 'There is something,' he said, finally. 'You know Sadie and I are coming to Kim's dinner party?'

'Huh?'

'You didn't know?'

'Oh,' I said. 'Yes. No. Yes. That's great.'

'You're okay with it?'

He was watching me closely.

George and Sadie are coming too? This is crazy!

'Of course,' I said. 'The more, the merrier. We'll have a fun night.'

My coffee arrived, and so did his. After George left, I got on the phone to Kim. 'What's this about George and Sadie coming to dinner?' I asked.

I could almost see Kim reddening over the phone.

'I'm sorry,' she said. 'I bumped into George on the street. It turns out he knows Adrian through some building work. Adrian mentioned dinner to him, and suddenly he and Sadie were invited.'

'This is wackadoodle insane,' I said. 'This is my ex-husband we're talking about.'

'Plus your new boyfriend,' Kim added.

'Todd's not my boyfriend! He's a friend! We've argued as

much as we've had good times!'

'Can you ever forgive me?'

'I suppose. But you must buy me a donut next time we go to the diner. You know Sandy has these new marshmallow and cherry donuts?'

'I know. I had one and had to run five kilometres to wear it off.'

'Yeah. Me too. Except without the running bit.' I took a long breath. Maybe I was overreacting to the dinner with George. We were all adults. And we'd moved on. Hadn't we? 'Are you busy tomorrow?'

'Only with being a librarian,' Kim said. 'I've been there so rarely of late that one staff member didn't recognise me.'

'Fame's overrated,' I told her. 'Keep tomorrow free. We're going out for apples.'

12

'Jacob Fobb?' I asked.

The man in the doorway was tall and lanky with piercing grey eyes. His hair was pushed back, thinning and straw brown.

I would have guessed his age to be around sixty, although he looked fit for his age.

'Yes?'

His voice was firmer, and now he was looking at us with something between suspicion and hostility.

'Rosie Ryan,' I said. 'I'm with the Gazette. And this is Kim. We're looking into the death of Hailey Lawrence, and I was told you might be able to help.'

Jacob grimaced. 'Who told you that?'

'Ian at Unicorn Books.' I smiled my most disarming smile. 'He speaks well of you and Plastic Apple.'

'The group was running a long time,' Jacob said. 'A lot of people came and went over the years.'

I nodded.

'The house is a mess,' Jacob continued.

I was sure it would more likely be starkly utilitarian than a mess. The front yard had been concreted over. Here and there, however, Mother Nature had rebelled. The concrete had cracked, and weeds sprung through like water bursting from a pipe. This incredible tribute to the art of landscape design seemed to stretch around the house. I'd spied a lap pool out the back, although I doubted he sat around it on sunny days and drank Pina Coladas. This must have been how he stayed healthy.

If the interior of his house was anything like this, it probably looked more like a Russian Gulag than an Australian suburban home.

Jacob's eyes strayed to Kim and then down to Trixie as if noticing her for the first time. 'Who's this?' he asked.

'This is Trixie.'

'Beagles,' Jacob said. 'My mother had one. Horrible woman. Nice dog.' He nodded to a nearby waist-high brick wall. 'I don't invite strangers into my house, but we can sit there.'

We followed him to the wall. Although he settled onto the top with no difficulty—maybe he sat there all the time—it wasn't so easy for me. Kim sat down, and I positioned myself between her and Jacob, feeling horribly like a piece of joinery on a house that had gone terribly wrong. Leaning back to appear casual, I flipped backward into the azalea bush behind.

'Goodness!' Jacob said as he and Kim picked me up. 'I've never seen anyone do that before.'

I smiled through clenched teeth. 'Sorry.' I shook leaves from my hair as I resumed my seat. 'I'm a big hit at children's parties. Now, what can you tell us about Plastic Apple?'

'Ah,' Jacob said, steepling his fingers. 'Plastic Apple. The group met more or less continuously from nineteen eighty-five to its last meeting three years ago. The original members met at the library, but the then owner of Unicorn Books offered to host them at the bookshop. The proprietor back then was Alice Coombes. Lovely lady. The group accepted, and that became their regular meeting place.'

'You mentioned lots of people came and went over the years,' I said.

'It's a natural thing.' Jacob seemed less weird now. Maybe he felt sorry for me after my somersault over the wall. 'Back in the old days, they had about twenty members. I've still got pictures from those meetings. A lot of people with long hair and beards.' He broke into an unexpected grin. 'Remember mullets?'

'The hairstyle?' Kim said, shuddering. 'Let's hope that fad doesn't return.'

'In the last years, the membership dropped until there were only half a dozen of us.'

I took out my notebook. 'And what do you write?' I asked.

'Family history.'

Kim nodded. 'I've seen you in the library's local history section,' she said. That was one of her specialties. 'You're a member of the genealogy society?'

'I've been researching my family for years. The Fobbs came here as convicts and settled in Cape Carson, Geelong, and Adelaide. I've been writing their histories.'

'You must have a lot of information by now.'

'I do. Not that anyone's ever wanted to publish it. What I've written is more of a collection of vignettes than anything else. Well researched, even if I say so myself, but there's no commercial market for it.'

'And the other members?' I asked. 'What did they write?'

'Well, there's Asher Vorback. He's a poet. You can ask him about his work.' Jacob rubbed his chin. 'Asher was with Plastic Apple from very early on. Looked different back then.'

'Not a mullet?' I said, in mock horror.

'Worse. *Long hair.* Anyway, Kylie was in the group for a long time too. Maybe twenty years.'

'What's Kylie's surname?'

'Crow. She was our resident romance writer.' Jacob paused. 'Fairly successful in what she does. Then there's Piper Ellis. Nice girl. Was with us for a few years. Wrote elven fantasy. That's fantasy fiction where the protagonists are elves. I'm not sure if she's still writing. Works at the visitor's centre. And, finally, there's Bella Lodley. She had her endless family saga she was working on: a series of books called The Dankworths.'

'What can you tell us about Hailey and Owen?' Kim asked.

He shifted his body uncomfortably. 'Hailey.' He said the name with distaste. 'Well, she didn't write that book, you know.'

'Oh?' I stared. '*The Second Death of Reginald Tanner*?'

'It was a collaborative effort. She brought that book to us every week for years, and we made *thousands* of suggestions. It was a horrible experience, listening to her honing and polishing that novel.' He sighed. 'She didn't know a verb from a noun. Hailey was pleasant but terribly ungrateful.'

Kim spoke up. 'When you say she didn't write it...'

'There was barely anything of her left in it by the time we'd all had our input. It started with a different title. Had a different beginning. Ending. Barely a sentence remained unchanged.' His face grew red. 'You'd think a young woman would be grateful for getting help from more experienced writers. But no, not Hailey Lawrence. She was happy to take all our ideas and drain us dry like the vampire in her novel.'

'Was there resentment about this?' I asked carefully. It was a stupid question: anger was written all over Jacob's face. 'From the members, I mean.'

Jacob snorted. 'I can't speak for the others,' he said. 'But that book should have had all our names on it. Especially mine.'

These last two words were spoken with such venom that even Trixie whined. I gave her a doggy snack. 'The story is that Hailey had depression and took her own life,' I said. 'What do you make of that?'

'I don't believe in depression. Everyone goes through hard times. People need to pick themselves up.'

That's easier said than done, I thought.

'So she never seemed unsettled?'

The man shrugged. 'I admit, sometimes she'd turn up at meetings like some tortured artist, clutching pages of her book. We'd spend half the meeting talking about how to improve her work. Hailey made the gatherings almost unbearable. It was all me, me, me. Then there was her mysterious email.' At our baffled expressions, he continued. 'I got an email purporting to be from her. Later, I realised it wasn't her email address, but I didn't notice then. The subject line read *Some Helpful Family History Information*.' He snorted. 'If only it were.'

'What was it?' Kim asked.

'A virus. I made the mistake of clicking on the attached file, and it immediately started scrubbing my hard drive. I lost about a year of research.'

'My goodness,' I said. 'That's terrible. But it wasn't from Hailey?'

He shrugged. 'She always said it wasn't, but I'm not sure

I ever believed her. Where did the sender get her name? If it wasn't Hailey, then who sent it?'

That was a good question. 'Can you tell us about the last meeting of Plastic Apple?' I asked.

'Well, there was a lot of animosity.'

'Really?'

'Hailey had already told us she had a publishing deal in the wind. That discussion had been going on for months. When she turned up that day, she said the deal was happening. They were publishing her book.'

'When was this meeting?' Kim asked. 'Do you recall?'

'Certainly. It was the day after the April Fool's Day earthquake. We had to move upstairs to the cookbook room because there was damage to the cellar.'

'And what was said at the meeting?'

'What wasn't said?' Jacob snorted. 'There was a huge fight, which is why it ended up being the last gathering of Plastic Apple. Hailey told us she was expecting a large advance for the book. Then she said something about how friendly the publisher had been. I'm sure I wasn't the only one to read between the lines.' When he saw the confused expression on our faces, he continued. 'The publisher was *too* friendly if you get my meaning.'

I frowned. 'Hailey was having a relationship with the owner of Lancelot Press?'

'It sounded that way, and half the group exploded over that.'

'Why?'

Jacob gave a dry chuckle. 'Hailey was an attractive girl,' he said. 'That's one reason why she got so much help from us. Owen Stamett was obsessed with her, and I mean *stalker* obsessed. I know that Hailey bumped into him on the street several times. Too many times, actually, as if he were orchestrating the meetings. Then there's Asher. Even then, he was old enough to be Hailey's father. Although he never said anything, he couldn't take his eyes off her at the meetings. And then he wrote poems about her.' He shook his head. 'His work was bad enough when he wrote about the bush and landscape. It was supposed to rhyme, although it never did. He started writing love poems about Hailey. They were awful. Simply dreadful.' He sighed. 'Maybe it's best that the club closed. There seemed to be a lot of bad luck surrounding the group, especially over those last months.'

'What do you mean?' Kim asked.

'Weird things happened. One of the side mirrors on my car got broken off. Hailey's dog died. Asher lost his phone and keys. Kylie's books at the library got vandalised. Piper ended up with a book in her bag that shouldn't have been there.'

I frowned. 'Goodness,' I said. 'That is strange.'

'And it all related to Plastic Apple?' Kim asked.

Jacob shrugged. 'The side mirror was broken off while I was

at a meeting,' he said. 'I was usually the first to arrive, so it could have been one of the other members. Asher was at the meeting both times when he lost things. Kylie was the most financially successful of us, and her books were ruined at the library. And Piper could have been accused of shoplifting.'

There seemed to be some omissions from the list. 'What about Bella?' I asked. 'And Hailey and Owen?'

'Bella's dog got bitten by Hailey's dog,' he said. 'I suppose that was bad luck. But then Hailey's dog died. The girl was upset by that.' He thought. 'Offhand, I don't remember anything happening to Owen. He led a charmed life, that boy.'

Maybe not too charmed, I thought. *He's missing, possibly dead.*

I gazed across the concrete to the fence beyond and the cerulean blue sky. A cloud passed across the sun, and I shivered. 'People say that Owen was responsible for Hailey's death,' I said. 'What do you think?'

'I don't know. Maybe. Like I say, Owen was obsessed with her. And you know he was in the army? Got kicked out. A *misunderstanding*, whatever that means. Then he was thrown out of the police force as well.' He shook his head. 'One thing I can tell you is that he had a violent nature.'

'What makes you say that?' Kim asked.

'He wrote sword and sorcery stuff like Conan the Barbarian. Hundreds and hundreds of pages jammed full of hacking and slashing. Killing people, dragons, giants, three-headed snakes. Anything that moved, his character killed.' He stopped. 'And Owen became quite strange after Hailey died. He thought someone was following him. Said he was getting weird calls from someone.'

'Hang-ups?'

'That's what he said. I saw him on the street one day, and suggested the calls could have been from Hailey's sister.'

'Rita?'

'Owen said she was certain Hailey didn't kill herself. She still believes it, I'm sure. Rita could have been harassing Owen.' He paused. 'Although, there's an even weirder explanation.'

I waited.

'Owen said the calls were coming from a private number. He thought it was *Hailey* calling him.'

'Hailey?' I said. 'But she was...'

'Dead? Yep. Owen said he thought Hailey was calling him from beyond the grave. It was driving him crazy. A few weeks later he disappeared.'

'Did he give any indication that he might be leaving town?' Kim asked.

'None. Truth is, I'm not even sure he did.' Jacob peered into the distance. 'You know, my mother used to believe in vengeful ghosts. She thought ghosts could come back and cause harm to the living. I never believed in any of that stuff until Owen disappeared. After it happened, though, even I wondered if he could have been murdered by Hailey's ghost.'

13

'Hailey Lawrence,' Kylie Crow said thoughtfully. 'That's a name I haven't heard in years.'

Kylie loved pink. The outside of her weatherboard house on Overside Drive was pink. So were the flowers in her garden. The interior walls of the building were pink. She had also decorated her shelves with ceramic pigs, which were pink. The coffee table around which we had tea and scones was pink. The teapot was pink, and so were the plates. About the only thing was wasn't pink were the scones and tea. If these could have been pink, I'm sure Kylie would have worked out a way to do it.

She was a squat, chubby woman with curly red hair and eyes that had the habit of narrowing into two tiny slits. They'd done that when Kim, Trixie, and I had arrived at her front door, and they did it again as she said Hailey's name.

'My goodness,' she said. 'How long is it since she died? Must be five years? Six?'

'Three,' I said. 'I understand you were both members of Plastic Apple.'

'Oh, that club. Well, yes, although I'm a professional writer. A romance author.' She lowered her voice conspiratorially. 'I was the most successful member of the group, although I never wanted to blow my own horn. Have you read my work?'

We shook our heads.

'I write librarian romance,' she said. 'Kim, you probably know me under the name of Sheila Makenthorpe.'

'Uh.' Kim managed to both nod and shake her head simultaneously. 'Okay.'

'You have some of my books in the library,' Kylie added.

'Oh yes. Of course.'

I spoke up. 'We understand you were in the group a long time.'

'Decades. It's inspiring to be surrounded by other writers. And we were always supportive of each other. Or mostly, anyway.'

'And Hailey?'

Kylie sighed. 'Hailey was young and foolish,' she said. 'And selfish. The whole group helped with that vampire book of hers, and she soaked it all up. Listened to everything we had to say. Month after month of advice and support. However, when we needed it to be reciprocated, she had very little to contribute.'

'Maybe she wasn't good at giving advice?'

'It was more than that. Hailey was self-obsessed. Always thinking of herself. Never wanting to help others. And that was only half of it. When she landed that publishing deal, you'd think she'd remember her friends.' Kylie vigorously shook her head. 'But—no. You ask her for a favour, and she wanted nothing to do with you.'

'What sort of favour?' I asked.

'Well...' Kylie shrugged. 'Hailey's deal was with Lancelot Press, and they have a line of romance novels. Now you'd think Hailey would have recommended an old friend to them. That's only fair.'

The woman stuck out her chin resolutely. That phrase *old friend* must have had a different meaning to Kylie than the rest of us.

'Goodness,' I said.

Kim sat up. 'We understand the last time the club met was just after the April Fool's Day earthquake,' she said. 'Can you tell us about that?'

Kylie Crow smirked. 'I remember the earthquake well,' she said. 'You know I work part-time for an accountant. The joke that day was, *did the Earth move for you*?' She laughed heartily as if no one had ever heard the pun before. 'You're right about meeting after the earthquake. That last time, we met in the cookbook room at Unicorn.'

'That last meeting,' Kim said. 'Do you remember what was discussed?'

'Well, of course, there was a lot of resentment aimed at Hailey. That's understandable, though. After she broke the news that her deal had been confirmed, it was like opening the floodgates. Everyone talked at once. Jacob was furious. He said Hailey had to share her book royalties with us.'

'Really?' I said. He hadn't mentioned that. 'I wonder how that would work.'

'I have no idea. It should have been all our names on that book, anyway. Then Asher was furious—which was hilarious. He's a funny little man. I'd never seen him angry before, but he turned bright red in the face and shook. He thudded his fist on the table. I thought he would explode.'

'He was angry about Hailey's book?'

Kylie shrugged. 'Later, he apologised to the rest of us for losing his cool. He said it was because of the money.' She lowered her voice. 'I knew better. Owen took Hailey's hand at one point. Sort of with excitement, although we all knew he was fixated with her. I saw Asher's eyes on them holding hands, and he looked ready to have a stroke.'

'Because Asher...'

'Asher was in love with Hailey—more than Owen, I think—and it was ridiculous. The man was close to retirement. Can you imagine a young girl wanting him? It wouldn't happen in a million years. Anyway, Asher almost exploded, which was fun to watch if you want to know the truth.'

'And the others?' Kim asked.

'Well,' Kylie considered. 'Piper was angry. She didn't trust Hailey for what happened with the book from the bookshop.' At our confused expressions, she continued. 'At the end of one meeting, Hailey happened to glance in Piper's bag and saw a book in there. Now, if we were going to buy books, we did it after the meeting. That meant Piper was stealing it. Hailey mentioned it, not to accuse her. I think it was surprise, more than anything else.'

'When did this happen?'

'A few months before. It was the meeting when Hailey first mentioned that she was talking to Lancelot Press about her book.'

'So what happened then?'

'Well, Hailey asked where the book had come from, and Piper said she didn't know. Piper went red in the face, and everyone was staring at her. We were all thinking the same: Piper was trying to steal the book. Anyway, Piper took it out. I'm sure she never forgot her embarrassment and the person who caused it. Piper was especially furious when Hailey told us the deal was happening and the advance would be big.'

'How big?'

Kylie smirked. 'Authors never mention exact figures,' she

said. 'But it was six figures, so it was large.' She examined her nails. 'Piper came out and said that Hailey had stolen everyone's ideas. So Hailey responded by saying that at least she wasn't a shoplifter.'

'Did Owen say much about Hailey's deal?'

'Not a lot. He was mostly trying to stop everyone from lynching her.'

'And Bella?'

'Bella was annoyed too, although she'd barely spoken to Hailey in months.'

'Why?'

'It went back...oh, must be a good year before that meeting. Hailey owned a dog. What was its name? Mister Brown. It was a terrier. And Bella owns a whippet named Mona. Mister Brown had bitten Mona, and that did not go down well with Bella.' Kylie frowned. 'Bella has a rather nasty side to her, I think. Anyway, Bella never forgave Hailey for it.' She paused. 'Now I'll tell you something, and I may be speaking out of turn.'

I nodded.

'Mister Brown died a few months later. Hailey told me she went into her yard and found him dead. The vet said he was poisoned. Hailey never accused Bella of it directly, but everyone wondered if she'd killed Hailey's dog.'

'My goodness,' Kim said. 'That's vindictive.'

'Bella's like that. Got a nasty streak to her.'

'We've been told there was some bad luck around the group,' I said.

'Bad luck?' Kylie repeated, thinking. 'That's one way of saying it. Asher lost his keys at one meeting and then his phone at the next. There was the incident with Piper and the book. Oh yes, Jacob and his car mirror and the mysterious email he got from Hailey that wasn't really from Hailey. Was there anything else?'

I prompted her. 'Was there something about your books at the library?'

'I'd forgotten about that. Yes, some very strange person scribbled through them. Mind you, I told the librarian on duty at the time, and they bought replacements.'

'Did anything happen to Bella?' Kim asked. 'Or Owen?'

'Not that I recall.'

'You mentioned Owen before,' I said. 'That he was fixated with Hailey.'

'Oh yes. I've written enough romance novels to tell when a man's got a crush on a woman—and he had it bad.'

'When Hailey died, Owen was the prime suspect,' I pointed out. 'Do you think Hailey killed herself? Or did Owen have something to do with it?'

Kylie hesitated. 'To be honest,' she said, 'it could be either. I've heard this story about Hailey having anxiety. I never saw it myself. She struck me as selfish and always out for herself. Could Hailey have had depression and jumped off that cliff? With a six-figure publishing deal around the corner? I doubt it.' She paused. 'Frankly, Owen being responsible was more plausible. He was strange after Hailey died. A couple of weeks later, I bumped into him on the street and he seemed overjoyed about something. Elated. I asked him what was happening, and he immediately tried to downplay it. But I knew something was up.'

What could that have been? I wondered. *Was it because Lancelot Press was interested in his book?*

'So he wouldn't say what it was?' I said.

'Only that he was looking forward to a business meeting.'

'And when was this?'

'A few days before he disappeared.' She frowned. 'I think he was meeting with his contact to arrange fake documents.'

'Fake documents?'

'You know. License. Passport. So he could start a new life under a different name.'

'I see.'

Kylie glanced at her watch. 'Now, I'd better get moving. I work for Dill and Crown in the mornings and do my writing in the afternoon. I don't make a fortune from my books, but they finance my yearly holiday to Canada. Love Canada. Go if you've never been.'

Kim and I got up to leave. 'Thanks for your time,' I said. 'If you think of anything else, please call me?'

'Of course.'

Kim, Trixie, and I returned to my jeep.

'Surely that business meeting was with the publisher,' Kim said.

'My thoughts, exactly. The possibility of a publishing deal gives this thing a whole new perspective. Owen would hardly do a runner knowing he was about to become a published author.'

'We need to follow up with the publisher.'

'And the other members of Plastic Apple.'

'But that can wait till tomorrow.' Kim smiled broadly. 'You haven't forgotten about tonight, have you?'

I groaned. 'I had kind of driven it from my mind.'

'Well, you shouldn't! Tonight, you, Todd, George, and Sadie are coming for dinner. We're having a party!'

14

'...talking about first cars,' Adrian said. 'Let me tell you about Donald.'

'Donald?' I said.

'My first car.'

We were seated around the dinner table at Kim's place. The evening had been a success, despite my misgivings. All the guests had turned up at much the same time to find Kim and Adrian busily cooking pasta and pizza on an industrial scale.

Adrian was a little taller than Kim. He was clean-shaven with a black crew cut and powerfully built; he managed an aged care facility in Cape Carson. But Adrian was also a great cook and had prepared most of the meal. His parents had owned an Italian restaurant when he was a kid.

George and Sadie had seemed relaxed the whole evening. Sadie was obviously a good influence on him. She was close to his age, pretty, and treated him with an equal measure of respect and firmness. I thought George needed that. He could be a little overbearing at times and needed a guiding hand to keep him on track.

While these two couples had been all over each other, I'd felt a little left out with Todd. He'd sat next to me and looked fabulous. Todd wore a white, open-necked shirt, tight jeans, and jacket. He had not touched me once during the night, not even with a stray elbow.

I felt somewhat let down by that elbow.

'Donald was my first car,' Adrian continued. 'An old Ford Laser. It would have been a good car in its day. Unfortunately, that day was long past.'

'And the reason you named it Donald?' I said.

'Named for the duck. You'll see why in a moment.'

'Did you pay for it yourself?' George asked.

'I did.' Adrian looked embarrassed. 'I worked part-time on a fishing boat. It was hard work and didn't pay much, but I liked it. Anyway, I ended up with a bunch of money. All the other kids were buying cars, or the lucky ones were gifted cars from their parents. My dad told me to wait till I had more money, but I thought, *What does he know? He's old!* So, I went out to buy this car and learned the biggest lesson of my life.'

'Which is?' Todd asked.

'You generally get what you pay for. Donald was a cheap car; I called it Donald because of the keyring. It had a tiny head of Donald Duck attached to it. You could push his nose, and it would light up.' He paused. 'As it turned out, that was about the only thing that worked. I drove this thing home and immediately found that the seat wouldn't stay upright. Every time I sat back, the seat fell backwards. I don't know how hoons recline in the driver's seat. I couldn't even see the road. I had to pull over and jam a pen into the seat adjuster to keep it upright.'

Sadie was laughing. 'Sounds challenging.'

'You haven't heard the worst of it. I had to use the horn, and it got stuck. So I was driving down the road with everyone staring at me. The only way I could turn it off was to stop the engine. Then I finally ended up on the highway. By then, I thought that I had only to get home. Then everything would be fine.

'But do you think I was that lucky? Oh no. It was a forty-two-degree Celsius day. Right in the heart of summer. Sitting bumper-to-bumper in a traffic jam, I'll never forget staring ahead and suddenly noticing vapour rising from the engine. Then I realised it wasn't vapour; it was steam pouring out from under the hood! I sat there, staring at it in horror. I had no idea what to do. I was a kid! Then a guy in the car beside me wound down his window and yelled, *Hey man! There's steam coming from your engine!* Adrian rolled his eyes. 'Like I hadn't noticed!'

By now, everyone in the room was laughing.

'So I sat there with this sense of gloom, knowing that I hadn't bought a car. I'd bought a lemon! I was sitting in a bona fide lemon. All my money had gone into it, and the thing was a pile of junk.'

'So what happened to the car?' I asked.

'Some guys helped push it to the side of the road. I had to ring my dad and confess what I'd done. He turned up—not too pleased—and we sold the car.'

'Did you get much for it?' Kim asked.

'About a quarter of what I paid.' Adrian shook his head. 'I wasted a lot of money that day.'

'I'm sure you did.' Kim smiled. 'But at least you got a good story out of it.'

Adrian laughed. 'It's an *expensive* story,' he said. 'It's a shame it makes me look dumb.'

'I don't think you're dumb at all.'

Kim touched his arm, and I felt a surge of happiness. Kim and Adrian were getting on like a house on fire. I glanced at Todd. He'd noticed the gesture too. He was smiling, but there was sadness in his expression.

What's he thinking about?

After dinner, George and Sadie left first, and then me and Todd a few minutes later. He'd driven us to Kim's place, and I got into his car feeling pensive. It was dark outside now, and the street was quiet.

'Kim looks so happy,' I said. 'It's lovely to see.'

'Sure.' Todd's response was short. 'Great.'

I didn't speak again until we arrived back at my place. After he pulled into my driveway, I turned to Todd. 'Hey you,' I said. 'Can you tell me what's wrong?'

'Nothing's wrong.'

'Are you still annoyed with me?'

'Wow, Rosie. You're amazingly perceptive. You really should be a private detective.'

I ignored Todd's sarcasm. 'Can I tell you how Hailey Lawrence's case is progressing?'

'I'm not sure you can call it a case when you're not a paid investigator.'

I continued anyway, telling Todd who it was that Kim and I had visited over the last few days. When I finished, he slowly nodded. 'So the writers' group were not Hailey's biggest fans?' he said. 'It sounds like there was more to the publisher than met the eye.'

'Lancelot Press? Because of Hailey's deal?'

'And the interest in Owen's book. I'm no expert on the publishing industry, but I imagine publishers are picky about who they publish. It seems odd that Lancelot was interested in books from two people who happened to be friends.'

I nodded. 'Any other thoughts?'

'Contact the other members of the writing group. Jealousy

is a classic motive for murder. Maybe one of them was so jealous of Hailey that they killed her. Owen could have been a red herring to throw us off track.'

I smiled. 'Thanks,' I said. 'That's helpful.'

'That's my job.'

15

The following day I was out of bed early and ready to continue contacting the remaining group members. I rang Kim to see if she was able to join me.

'You're in luck,' she said. 'Adrian and I were going on a picnic, but he's been called into work.'

'I'll meet you at Sandy's?'

'Sure.'

Soon, I was nestled into one of the booths at Sandy's as the owner handed me my first jumbo double-shot caramel latte for the day.

'That should wake you up,' she said.

I took a long sip from the cup. 'Yep,' I said as the caffeine took hold. 'I'm awake.'

She grinned. 'By the way, do you know the rock and roll festival is definitely a goer? The council's given approval, and our committee is working through the details.'

'Fantastic. When's it happening?'

'Early summer.'

'I'll come to one of your committee meetings and get some info.'

Kim came rushing in the door. 'Hey Rosie!' she said. 'Is it a beautiful day or what?'

Sandy and I exchanged glances. The morning was overcast, and scattered showers threatened.

'She's in love,' I explained.

'Ha!' Sandy said as she hurried off to make Kim's coffee. 'That explains everything!'

Kim sat opposite. 'So,' she said, lowering her voice. 'What do you think of Adrian?'

'He seems nice.'

'When you say nice, do you mean *really* nice or *moderately* nice or *a bit* nice—'

I laughed. 'Adrian's fantastic!' I assured her. 'The most amazing new boyfriend anyone's ever had in the history of the human race!'

'Do you really think so?' Kim's coffee arrived, and she took a long sip. 'He's very polite and kind. Adrian's been living with his mum because she's unwell. He also helps out at the hospital bookshop.'

'You don't need to convince me,' I said, shaking my head. 'Now, are you ready to do some investigating?'

'Absolutely!'

Half an hour later, we were standing outside the home of Asher Vorback. It was a Japanese-inspired place, flat-roofed with curving gutters. Cherry blossoms dotted a front yard clad in white pebbles and enclosed by bamboo fencing. A water feature gurgled adjacent to the house.

We knocked on the door and waited. It only took a moment for a balding, short man with a round face to answer. We quickly explained the purpose of our visit.

'The death of Hailey Lawrence?' Asher said. 'Why are you digging up old dirt on that?'

Kim explained. 'Hailey's sister, Rita, has asked us to investigate.'

'There's not much I can say—'

I spoke up. 'Other members of Plastic Apple have spoken to us,' I said. 'It's important to hear your side of the story.'

He raised an eyebrow. 'What have they been saying?'

'It's probably best if we speak inside.'

Asher reluctantly invited us in, asking that we take our shoes off at the door and that we leave Trixie outside. He owned a cat who didn't get along with dogs.

Inside, minimalism was the order of the day, and the layout of everything had been carefully designed. A single artwork of a snow-covered mountain top sat precisely in the middle of a wall. The coffee table in the living room was bare, and everything was fastidiously clean.

'You have a lovely home,' I said.

'Thanks. It's not to everyone's taste. I like order and organisation. Must come from working at the council for so long. I'm in the Tenders and Procurement department. Every *i* has to be dotted and *t* crossed.'

We sat around the coffee table. A Siamese sauntered in, regarded us suspiciously, and disappeared through another doorway. 'That's Sapphire,' he said. 'Don't be offended. She hates everyone equally.'

'You've been there a while?' I asked.

'Thirty-three years. Not that I'm counting.' He rubbed his chin. 'So Rita's still wondering about Hailey's death. It always seemed cut and dried to me.'

'How so?'

'Owen killed her. He was fixated with Hailey. Couldn't keep his eyes—or hands—off her. I almost went to the police to report him as a stalker. Wish I had now. Hailey might still be alive.'

'Her death was ruled a suicide,' Kim pointed out.

'There was the suicide note,' Asher agreed reluctantly. 'But it was implausible, don't you think? A woman types a suicide note before killing herself. And she was about to become a published author *and* fly off on an overseas holiday?'

'Did you ever see any sign of Hailey's anxiety?' I asked.

'Sometimes. Frankly, one time I saw her on the street, and

she looked very unwell. She was shaking and upset. I asked her what was wrong, and she put it down to nerves.'

'But you still don't think she killed herself?'

Asher shook his head resolutely. 'Absolutely not,' he said. 'That last time I saw her, she was positive and upbeat. Looking forward to seeing her book in print.'

'When was that?' Kim asked.

'About a week after the last Plastic Apple meeting.'

'Can you tell us about that last meeting?'

Asher sighed. 'It was just after the earthquake. The April Fool's Day quake.'

'We've been told there was an argument at the meeting.'

'I suppose you could call it that. Hailey was excited when she arrived. When she told everyone about the deal, the whole atmosphere changed.'

'Why?' I asked.

'It was the book.' Asher reddened. 'Frankly, everyone contributed to that novel. We were happy to do it. I mean, that's the purpose of the writing group. To make suggestions. To give feedback. The problem was, with Hailey, it went on for years. People were sick and tired of hearing about it. Then she waltzed in the door and said she was signing a six-figure deal. It set everyone off.' He paused. 'We liked her, though. She was a nice person. That's why we helped her.'

'But when she got the publishing deal—'

'People felt betrayed. Not me. I'm a poet. There's no money in poetry. I know that.' He shook his head. 'Poor Hailey. To make matters worse, she mentioned a holiday to Europe. It was like rubbing salt in the wound. Anyway, Jacob was furious. He said Hailey should share her royalties with the group. Then there was Owen, drooling over Hailey. It was as if she'd turned up in a bikini. It was revolting to watch. And Bella hadn't been Hailey's biggest fan for a long time. Not since her dog was bitten.'

'Can you tell us what happened?'

'Mona is Bella's dog, and Hailey's dog bit it. Bella never forgave her. People get touchy about their pets.' He leaned close. 'I'd hurt anyone who harmed my little Sapphire. Cats and dogs are better than people in many cases.'

'They can be true friends,' I agreed. 'And how was Kylie?'

'Furious—but for a completely different reason. Kylie asked Hailey if she could recommend her to Lancelot Press. And Hailey said no! No wonder Kylie was irate! She's a published author. Romance novels. Not my choice, but each to their own.' He rubbed his chin. 'Who have I left out?'

'Piper?' Kim prompted.

'Oh yes. Well, there was that whole issue about the stolen book. Hailey had spotted it in Piper's bag, and Piper denied knowing anything about it. The poor girl went bright red when Hailey pointed it out. Piper was embarrassed. You could tell. It was a shame Hailey didn't have the sense to hold her tongue and mention it when no one else was around.'

'Any thoughts about how it got there?' I asked.

Asher hesitated. 'Frankly,' he said, 'I've always suspected Bella.'

'Why?'

'She's got a—how would you put it—sly side to her. You can even see it in her face. A nastiness. It could all be in my imagination, but odd things happen when she's around.'

'Like what?'

'Well, I told you about Bella's dog. A few months after that, Hailey's dog got poisoned. Did Bella do it? I don't know. Then there was the email Jacob got from Hailey, but she always denied sending it. One of Jacob's car mirrors got damaged, too, although that kind of thing happens. It could be a coincidence. And someone vandalised Kylie's books at the library.'

'Which is silly,' Kim said. 'We usually replace damaged books. Especially if the author's popular.'

'Like I say, this could all be nothing. Coincidence. Accidents happen. People vandalise books. Except it seemed to happen a lot when Bella was around. An awful lot. That's why I was always standoffish with her. Best to keep a little distance between yourself and Bella Lodley.'

I spoke up. 'I understand you lost some items while you were a member? Keys and a phone?'

'Oh yes. I'd forgotten about them.'

'Nothing happened to Owen?' Kim said.

'Not that I know of,' he said. 'Although he could have been behind the vandalism, he didn't seem the kind. Forgive me for saying this, but he was a dumb oaf. A *dangerous* oaf, I think. You've probably heard about his history with the police force and the army. I'm inclined to think that he would simply punch someone in the nose rather than do things behind their back.'

'Asher,' I said. 'Forgive me for saying this, but it sounds like there was a lot of bad feeling in the group. Why did you stay a member?'

'For a lot of reasons. The feedback was good. That's scarce among non-writers. People writing for a while can suggest ways to fix writing problems.' He stopped and thought. 'And Plastic Apple was a lot of fun. Sure, there were dysfunctional people in the group. That didn't stop us from coming together and having good times. Christmas parties. Birthdays. Even picnics.' He paused reflectively. 'It's a shame it all came to an unhappy end.'

'And the bookshop must have been a wonderful location,' Kim added.

'Better than wonderful,' Asher said, suddenly smiling. 'And you know the best thing of all? It's open every day of the year!'

16

'Rosie,' Barry said. 'You *must* help us.'

We were sitting on the outside terrace at the Kilkenny Arms. It was late the following morning and Barry had rung me to request a meeting. I peered out across the sparkling bay. There were a thousand things I wanted to do. At the top of my list was continuing my investigation into the death of Hailey Lawrence. Close to the top of my list—along with winning the lottery and meeting the man of my dreams—was avoiding AFSA as much as possible.

I took a sip of my coffee. 'I'm not sure I can.'

'But you can,' Barry said eagerly. 'You're an investigator. I've asked people about you, Rosie. You've helped to solve some high-profile cases. We need someone like you.'

'To do what—exactly?' I asked.

'To find the relic, of course.'

I nodded, not replying. It was like saying he wanted help recovering the lost Ark of the Covenant. Or locate the city of

Atlantis.

'Rosie,' Barry said patiently. 'We know you're one of us, otherwise you wouldn't have agreed to be our guest of honour.'

There were a lot of things I could say about that. The first was that my ordinarily efficient editor had made a complete stuff-up and volunteered me for the wrong organisation. I should have been hanging out with Nan and the other old ladies while they discussed the benefits of cross stitch. Instead, I was with the UFO nuts who thought dead aliens were being stored in a place called Zone Nine.

'I...' My voice trailed away. Could I help find their relic? There couldn't have been many people with access to Barry's hotel room. Only a handful of hotel staff. And the police were unlikely to look into the theft too seriously. Todd and the other cops had bigger fish to fry than to chase alien artifacts. Then there was my destruction of Laniakea. It had been a thing of beauty until I'd annihilated it. Surely I owed them something for destroying the universe.

'All right,' I agreed reluctantly. 'I can't promise anything, but I'll make some inquiries.'

'Thank you, Rosie,' he said. 'I'll let the others know you're on the job.'

I nodded without speaking. Sure. Rosie Ryan in her next feature film: *Raiders of the Lost Alien Relic*.

It did *not* have a ring to it.

After finishing my coffee, I searched for the hotel manager and found Natalie Cook in her office at her computer.

'We rarely have thefts,' Natalie said when I asked about the robbery. I'd interviewed her a few times over the years. Her usually cheerful smile had been replaced by a frown. 'The last one was almost a year ago.'

'How would the thief get into the room?' I asked. 'Who has the keys?'

She hesitated. 'The room hirer, of course,' she said. 'We also have another key at the desk. Housekeepers have master keys. There's a list.'

'Can I speak to them?'

'Of course. Although the police have already interviewed them, you may discover something they didn't.'

The next few hours were spent tracking down the housekeepers working the day the relic had been stolen. A team of three usually did the floors, one at a time.

'I remember Mister Rycroft's room,' Manny said. She was a slim twenty-something-year-old with short, black hair. We were down in the hotel's laundry room. 'It was tidy, and I gave it one of our ten-minute spruce-ups. Changed the linen. Cleaned the bathroom. Replaced the toiletries.'

'What time was this?'

She shrugged. 'Between ten and eleven.'

The ASFA attendees were on a break at that time. Any of them could have stolen the relic.

'Do you remember seeing anything unusual?'

'Aliens under the bed?' Manny smiled. 'No. Nothing like that.'

'Did you touch his bags?'

'There was no need. They were sitting over to one side, under a window.'

'You know it was an alien...object that went missing.' I described it. 'Did you see anything like that in the room?'

She answered *no*.

'Okay,' I said. 'And anyone unusual on that level? Other guests or someone who shouldn't have been there?'

She frowned. 'There were a few people,' she said. 'A young woman with pink hair. And the man who was accused.'

That's Neo and Jasper, I thought.

'And where were they?' I asked.

'The woman was going into her room,' Manny said, thinking. 'And the man was heading into the elevator.'

'Anyone else?'

'No.'

This didn't mean a whole lot. The Kilkenny Arms was a nice hotel—the best in town—but it wasn't a fortress. Anyone could have wandered up there, broken into Barry's room, and taken the relic. I thanked Manny for her time and returned to the reception desk. Natalie had given me permission to view the security footage. It wasn't a job I was looking forward to; having Kim with me would have made the job more fun. Unfortunately, she had to be at work.

I settled into the tiny security office of the Kilkenny Arms. It was a dark room with a bank of monitors, a desk, a chair, and little else. A person with claustrophobia wouldn't have lasted five minutes. I examined the recordings. The only camera of any use was the one monitoring the door to the ground floor stairwell.

Trawling through the video when the relic was taken wasn't an easy task. Most people in the footage were strangers; there were, after all, two conferences taking place. Most of the hotel guests were UFO or fabric enthusiasts; sadly, neither wore signs identifying themselves as either.

Just as I was about to give up, I spotted a figure dash across the lobby.

What took my attention wasn't anything in particular. It was simply that he was a stranger to the hotel. I watched as he crossed to the stairs. Switching to another monitor, I saw him disappear up the stairs and return a few minutes later with a parcel under his arm.

'Bingo,' I murmured.

Trixie whined, and I patted her head.

The man walked back across the lobby and exited the building.

That's got to be him, I thought.

I rewound the footage, taking several screen captures and printing the images. My next difficulty was in identifying him. The man had purposely hidden his appearance.

He wore a striped shirt, jeans, and a baseball cap down low. I hadn't spotted him on any other footage, so he wasn't a guest. He could have been anyone.

I showed the images to Natalie and the other staff. No one recognised him, so I ended up leaving the hotel feeling both elated and challenged.

'Okay,' I said to Trixie. 'This must be the guy. Now we've got to work out his identity. If we can do that, we can track him down and retrieve the relic.'

I was feeling more like Indiana Jones with each passing moment. Trixie and I went to the businesses surrounding the hotel, asking if anyone knew the man in the picture. It was at the Thai restaurant across the road where I hit paydirt.

'He's come in here,' Jack Tyler, the owner of Cape Thai confirmed. 'A few evenings this week.'

'Do you know his name?'

'No.'

'Does he pay by cash or card?'

'I'm not sure,' he said. 'I'm pretty sure I know where he lives, though.'

'Really?' My heartbeat went up. 'Where's that?'

The manager frowned. 'Can you tell me what this is about?'

I explained about the robbery.

'I suppose I can tell you,' he said. 'Though I should mention that he might not even be a guy.'

'He could be a she?'

'It's hard to say. He—or she—keeps their baseball cap down so low I can't tell. And their voice is a little high. I honestly don't know.'

'So where do you think he lives?'

'My home is on Crescent Drive at the back of town. You know the street? Anyway, he's been coming out of a place halfway down the block. It's a rundown timber joint. A real dive. I'm sure that's him. He rides a motorcycle.'

After thanking him, I headed to my jeep and jumped in with Trixie. I rang Kim and told her what I'd achieved. She listened in silence until I finished.

'Okay,' she said slowly. 'So now you're heading off to see Todd, and then he and a bunch of cops will go pay this guy a visit.'

I groaned. 'You know what Todd's like,' I said. 'He'll say there's no evidence.'

'Well, maybe it's not him. Anything could have been in that parcel.'

'He was hiding his identity.'

'He might always dress like that.'

This argument could go on forever. I hated it when Kim was like this. It was as if she had a blind spot about her own stubbornness. 'Okay,' I said. 'Fine. It could be anyone. He could be Harold Holt for all we know.'

'I doubt it. Harold Holt was Australia's seventeenth prime minister and vanished while swimming in 1967.'

'Maybe he was kidnapped by aliens!' I snapped. 'That's what my UFO buddies would say! Anyway, this guy needs to be checked out, and that's what I'm doing.'

'Rosie—'

But I'd already hung up.

17

Trixie and I slowly drove down Crescent Drive.

It was late in the day now, and I was feeling impressed with myself. In only a few hours, I'd tracked down the person who stole AFSA's alien relic. I had only to identify the house, and it would be case closed.

My eyes scanned the buildings.

House after house was typically suburban: well-trimmed lawns, picket fences, weatherboard or brick homes. I'd begun to think that Jack from the Thai restaurant had made a mistake when my focus narrowed on an overgrown garden. Although the house wasn't a wreck, it was obviously unloved.

I stopped my jeep and climbed out.

Trixie whined.

'Everything's fine,' I said. 'We're just taking a look.'

The fence along the front was unpainted, as was the house beyond. The lawn was long, and the shrubs overgrown. The house could have been someone's holiday home. My eyes scanned the windows. There was no sign of anyone inside, and no motorcycle in the driveway either.

This looks safe enough, I thought.

I went to the front door and tried peering into the windows facing the lawn, but gauze curtains blocked my view. Despite my trepidation at meeting the thief, I had to establish that this was his lair. I knocked at the door and waited. After a minute, when there was no answer, I tried the handle.

Locked.

Traipsing around the side of the house, I peered into windows without success. The same gauze curtains were behind the glass. Finally reaching the back door, I glanced inside to see an old sunroom with dated furnishings. I tried the door handle. The door opened freely.

'Hello?' I called.

My nerves were on edge as I half-expected the thief to come barrelling out of a hallway. I called out again and waited. No reply. Slowly, I crept across the sunroom and up the hall. No sign of life. Maybe this was simply someone's holiday home with an unlocked door.

I called out again and received no reply. The air was still and quiet. Trixie whined.

'It's okay, girl. We're just taking a look around.'

I methodically searched each bedroom —and it wasn't without some sense of guilt. Kim and Todd had rebuked me on a dozen occasions for breaking into people's homes. My only answer was that it was for a good cause.

And this was one of those times! I was a heroic adventurer on a quest to find a stolen MacGuffin! That's what movie lovers called the object of the hero's quest—a MacGuffin!

Except I wasn't having much luck. The first two bedrooms were empty, and the house seemed undisturbed. The living room at the end was sparsely furnished with a television, a tattered lounge, and a square table surrounded by four timber chairs.

The third bedroom led from the living room and—

Bingo.

Someone had been here. There was a laptop and a backpack with some loose pages beside it. My eyes turned to a green recycled shopping bag sitting on the bed. I crossed to it and peered inside.

My heart gave a leap of pure joy. Even Trixie whined. The alien relic, artifact, or whatever the UFO people wanted to call it, sat inside. I gripped the object in my hands. It was lighter than I'd imagined. Barry had said it was mostly aluminium, and it felt like it. I returned it to the bag.

'We did it,' I told Trixie.

She whined again, and this time I recognised the worried sound in her throat. Turning, I glimpsed a figure in the doorway and a masked face. Something swung through the air, collided with my head, and Trixie's frenzied barking filled my world. Then there was dead silence and darkness.

When I awoke, the first thing I saw was late afternoon light filtering through the curtains in the front room. I tried moving my hands, but they were tied behind me, and tape was across my mouth. I was tied to a chair in the living room.

Trixie's anxious barking was coming from the bedroom that contained the backpack and laptop. At least she was okay. The rest of the building sounded silent and still. My attacker was gone.

This is another fine mess I've gotten myself into.

I angled my head back, and a sting of pain rocketed through my skull. Fortunately, I was alive, but that was only because my attacker had chosen not to kill me. That wasn't part of his—or her—plan. They intended to incapacitate me, and they'd done an excellent job of it. I pushed against my bonds. The rope was tight and, judging by the feel of it, attached to the chair's timber legs. Likewise, my legs were secured firmly to the chair's front legs.

I'm an idiot.

Kim had said not to come here. She'd even told me to tell Todd, and I'd ignored her. Why didn't I listen? Todd would have followed up my investigation in a heartbeat. So why didn't I contact him?

Because he would have chastised me for doing police work.

Anger rose to my cheeks.

But that's what I did! I was an investigative reporter. It was my job to follow up on leads!

Goodness, I thought. *This is silly. I'm wasting my time getting irate when the person who attacked me could return at any moment.*

I had to get free. Experimentally straining against the rope around my wrists seemed to achieve little; if anything, they seemed to tighten.

I wriggled the chair experimentally. Although it was timber, it was obviously cheaply constructed from a flat pack. If I could get one leg free, it might give me enough movement to break the whole seat.

Easing myself forward, I could stand a few inches with the chair still attached. A good whack diagonally across the base might loosen the timber. I edged to the side of the room and took a deep breath. If I didn't do this right, I might hurt myself badly. I took a few more breaths and smacked the chair's back left corner against the wall. It achieved nothing—besides causing a slight dent in the gyprock.

Oh dear, I thought. *Now I'm a vandal.*

Still, there was no other way around this. Lifting the chair again, I struck the same back corner against the wall. I lifted the chair and moved back a foot. Then I repeated the action again. And again. And again. It became a rhythm. Lift. Whack. Lift.

Whack. Lift. Whack.

Sweat was rolling down my face as the gag in my mouth grew sodden.

Come on, I thought, as frustration kicked in. *Come on. I've got this!*

With one almighty effort, I threw myself and the chair back into the wall. There was a huge crack, and then the chair toppled. I screamed through the gag as the chair—with me on it—crashed to the floor.

The pain that shot through my right shoulder was horrible. I felt like bursting into tears. My shoulder wasn't broken, but I'd jolted it badly. I experimentally moved my body and felt some give.

Wait a minute...

That collision with the floor *had* snapped something that—fortunately—wasn't part of my anatomy. I jammed my legs against the base of the chair. There was definitely movement, so I continued this motion again. Pushing left and right until something disconnected from behind. Despite my hands still being tied to the timber uprights, they were looser than they'd been.

I wriggled my body wildly, pushing against what remained of the piece of furniture. One leg broke. Then the rear cracked free. Although I was still attached to the timber, at least now I could almost get my hands free of the wood. I felt like the shattered mast and rigging of a damaged sailing ship.

A shape moved at the window.

I froze, staring at it in horror. Was this my attacker? Had he come back to finish the job? I wriggled desperately against the ropes. There was rattling at the door. Trixie broke into frenzied barking.

No! I thought. *This isn't fair! I'm almost free!*

There was a sound at the back door. It creaked open. There were voices. Footsteps. And then—

'Rosie!' Kim cried.

She and Todd, and other police officers poured into the room. I let out a gasp of relief as Kim untied the gag. Todd dragged the mess of timber and rope free before helping me to my feet. A cop opened the door to the bedroom, and Trixie came bounding out.

I dropped to my knees and quickly examined her. She was fine. I stood up to face Todd and Kim's concerned faces. I didn't know what to say. It was only a matter of time before their relief would turn to anger.

'Anyone feel like coffee?' I gasped. 'I'm dying for a cup.'

18

'One of these days,' Todd said grimly, 'other people won't be there to rescue you.'

Kim, Todd, and I were sitting in a booth at Sandy's Diner. It was evening, my shoulder was aching, and I had a cut on my leg from splintered wood. The coffee was helping to divert my attention from the pain. Equally diverting was the unhappy response from my friends.

'Okay,' I said. 'I was an idiot. I shouldn't have gone there alone. I could have gotten killed.'

'And Trixie, too,' Kim said.

That made a huge lump in my throat. 'Yep,' I said as tears threatened. 'And Trixie, too. But I'm okay, and so is Trixie. Now, what have you found in the house?'

This last question was aimed at Todd. 'Not a whole lot,' he said. 'The place has been emptied. The bag and other belongings you mentioned are gone. Besides some empty food cans in the kitchen trash, the place is clean.'

'And fingerprints?'

'I've got some forensics people checking for prints. Don't hold your breath, though. Whoever did this was smart. The back door was expertly picked, and none of the other neighbours noticed this person coming or going. You're lucky that Jack Tyler made that connection.'

'So the thief was living there?'

Todd frowned. 'I think it was only a base of operations. None of the beds have been slept in.'

'I saw the relic,' I said, frustrated. 'It was there. I picked it up. I held it in my hands.'

'Rosie,' Kim said. 'You don't even believe in this stuff. Why were you so determined to track this thing down?'

'Because I broke the universe!' I said. 'The UFO people spent a *year* building it, and I wrecked it in ten seconds! You'd feel guilty too!'

Todd rolled his eyes. 'Sounds like a great reason to put your life at risk,' he said.

'Todd—' He was seriously annoyed. Now wasn't the time to get into a debate. 'I'm sorry.'

'Rosie,' he said. 'I've only known you for six months and in that time you've committed multiple break and enters. Anyone else, I would have arrested. I didn't because of our friendship.' His face darkened. 'Now I'm wondering if I've been making a serious mistake. You clearly have no idea what constitutes an illegal act.'

'What can I say—'

He held up a hand. 'Next time I catch you breaking into someone's home,' he said, 'I'm arresting you. I don't care if it's for an article or you're investigating a crime. Are we clear?'

I nodded. 'As crystal.'

Todd stood. 'I'll let you know what we find.'

He left, and I turned to Kim. 'That was a bit rough,' I said.

'Rosie!' Kim said. She looked ready to explode. 'Are you joking? You could be dead! What if the guy had killed you instead of tying you up?'

'Then I'd be dead,' I mumbled. She looked ready to walk out too, so I quickly changed the subject. 'Are you free tomorrow? I want to visit Piper and Bella.'

'Can you guarantee that we won't be attacked and tied up? Or murdered?'

'I can't promise anything,' I said, finishing my coffee. 'But it's improbable that more than one person wants me dead in a week.'

'I don't know,' Kim said. 'I'm thinking about joining the queue myself.'

She reluctantly agreed to join me. Soon, I was stumbling in the front door of my home to find Nan sitting on the lounge watching TV.

'You're late!' she declared. 'And what happened to you?

You're limping?'

'Just another day on the job.'

Nan frowned. She knew me better than I knew myself. 'Haven't been doing anything silly?' she said. 'Have you?'

'Not at all.'

After making cups of tea for both of us, I settled onto the lounge beside her.

'How's it going with that nice policeman?' Nan asked after a while.

'Todd? He's a pain in the posterior.'

Nan sighed. 'You two should have been married by now. You need to let your guard down a little. Have a little give. You're too rigid. Come to yoga with me sometime. It'll do you the world of good.'

'I'll think about it,' I said. 'I also need to lose some weight.' Kim had been encouraging me to get into an exercise program. Those extra kilos I'd put on over winter wouldn't disappear without some effort. 'Is there anything for dessert?'

'Ice cream and apple pie.' She grinned. 'It's low fat.'

'Yep. And pigs might fly.'

The next day, I picked Kim up early to visit Piper Ellis. The woman worked in the Cape Carson tourist office, a small building at the east end of the beach. Racks of leaflets and maps of the area lined the walls. A video of local tourist high-lights played in the corner. Piper was in her mid-twenties, with straight brown hair and a small nose. She had one of those faces that was easily forgotten. Piper had just served a tourist when we marched in the door.

'Hailey Lawrence?' Piper said nervously after we explained the purpose of our visit. 'I don't know if I can tell you much. It's been so long.'

'Any help would be much appreciated.' I pushed on. 'We understand you were a member of Plastic Apple. Can you tell us about that?'

Piper frowned. 'I was only a member for a few years,' she said. 'I barely knew anyone.'

That had to be untrue. I wondered why she was lying. 'What did you think of the group?' I asked.

'I'd rather not say.'

Her easily forgotten face frowned.

'Piper,' I began. 'We've spoken to Jacob, Asher, and Kylie. They all had things to say about each other. And you. It's important to get your side of the story.'

'What did they say about me?'

I didn't answer. 'Was the group helpful?' I asked, keen to stay in control of the conversation.

'I've been writing since I was young,' Piper said. 'I've always wanted to be an author.' She glanced about self-consciously as if afraid her employer would hear her desire for a career change. 'I read everything by Tolkien, Feist, McCaffrey. They inspired me to create my own world where my characters go on quests, battle giants and dragons.' She paused. 'Plastic Apple helped. People always had suggestions.'

'And how's the book going?' Kim asked.

'Good. It's taking a while.'

'Lots of editing?' I asked.

She looked embarrassed. 'It never ends,' she said. 'I fix something, and then I see another bit I want to change.'

I smiled. 'Good things take time,' I said. 'I believe Jacob was the club president? What was his writing like?'

'He wasn't the club president. We weren't that organised. As far as his writing went, it was fine. He was writing his family history. They came to Australia as convicts.' She lowered her voice. 'To tell you the truth, it was all a little boring. I mean, the historical stuff was fine, but they never did anything. They were all mine workers and laborers.' Piper stopped again. 'He was nice enough, though he always wanted to be in charge of the group. Did all the organising with Ian about using the room. You know he's the owner of Unicorn Books?'

'Yep.'

'I still go there all the time.'

'And what did you think about the other members?'

Piper shrugged. 'Kylie was always pleasant,' she said. 'She writes romance novels. I didn't enjoy workshopping them, to tell you the truth. They were always friends-to-enemies kind of stuff. Still, she's made money out of it. Financed her overseas holidays with her writing.' She thought. 'Then there's Bella. A snob, I thought. She had that awful series she was writing.'

'What was it about?' I asked.

'The Dankworths,' Piper said, rolling her eyes. 'It was this long family saga across five generations. Everyone was constantly backstabbing each other over grain fields and sheep stations. She had three books written with more to come.'

'And you didn't like them?' Kim said.

'There wasn't a single likeable person in the whole saga. Everyone was always arguing. There were murders. Thefts. It was more an organised crime gang than a family tale.'

'And Asher?' I asked. 'What did you think of him?'

Piper sighed. 'Look,' she said. 'He was basically a good guy. Helped keep the peace in the meetings.' She hesitated. 'Maybe I shouldn't say...'

We waited.

'All right,' Piper continued. 'Asher was madly in love with Hailey. It was gross, really, because Hailey was my age. There was something like a thirty-year age gap between them. I felt like throwing up when he took her hand or touched her shoulder. Asher is a poet. Or that's what he calls himself. He wrote all this terrible Australian poetry in the style of Henry Lawson, but it never rhymed. We'd all listen politely, but it was clear he was awful. There was always kind of an odd silence when he finished reading.' Her face darkened. 'So it was pretty hard to take. And Owen was just as stupid. He was madly in love with Hailey too.'

For a second, anger flashed across Piper's face. Her eyes filled with something approaching rage.

Maybe even something beyond that.

Realisation struck me. 'You were in love with Owen,' I said.

Piper stared at me. 'No,' she said, reddening. 'I..I was just...'

'He was a handsome guy,' I continued quickly, keen to keep her talking. 'I can't fault your taste.'

'It's just that...' Piper faltered. 'Well, he was *nice*. And good. And always helped me with my book. Owen wrote sword and sorcery books, and I did elven fantasy. They're similar genres. We understood each other.' Her eyes grew watery. 'I did like him. I hoped...well, it's not important. He loved Hailey.'

'Did he tell you that?'

'Not then. I discovered later.'

Kim spoke up. 'Some people hold Owen responsible for Hailey's death.'

'Owen would never hurt anyone.' Piper's mouth turned down. 'He was a kind person.'

'He was kicked out of the army for fighting,' Kim pointed out. 'And left the police force under a cloud.'

Piper shook her head resolutely. 'It makes no difference,' she said. 'He told me one day that he regretted his past.'

'This was at one of the meetings?'

'No. I bumped into Owen on the coastal walk one day. He was excited. Pleased. He'd gotten word that a publisher was interested in his book: the same publisher as Hailey.'

I thought back to the letter Owen had received. It was only a few days before his death.

'And he seemed fine?' I said.

'He was elated. Over the moon. We even discussed Hailey and her death, and he said he was coming to terms with it.' Piper faltered. 'That's when Owen admitted he'd been in love with her. Although he was devastated when she killed herself, Owen said the publisher contacted him because of Hailey.'

'So she recommended him to Lancelot Press?'

'She must have. That's why it makes no sense that he would harm Hailey.'

'Do you believe Hailey killed herself?'

'I don't know. All I know is that she wasn't a nice person.'

'What makes you say that?'

'One day, she burst out laughing when Kylie was reading from her work. Although romance novels might not be everyone's cup of tea, it's rude to laugh at someone's writing. And then there were Asher's poems. Generally, he was not very good. Then one day, Asher turned up with something good. Excellent, really.'

'And?'

'Hailey said she thought it sounded like a poem by Henry Lawson. She said she'd studied a piece like it at high school. Asher went bright red, said it may have been similar, and shoved it away in his bag.' She paused. 'When I got home, I checked the poem, and it was identical.'

Plagiarism, I thought. *That must have embarrassed Asher terribly.*

'We understand the other members of Plastic Apple were unhappy with her getting the publishing deal,' Kim said.

Piper hesitated. 'That last meeting was awful,' she said. 'That's why the club self-destructed.'

'Can you tell us about it?'

The young woman didn't speak for a moment. She peered out at the beach. 'I suppose the others have already told you what happened,' she said. 'We were meeting in the cookbook room. The cellar was out of action because of the earthquake. Poor Ian. He'd already had to do repair work on it the previous year. On the day of the last Plastic Apple meeting, there was a *Danger* sign and rope barrier across the stairs, and a notice saying we had to meet in the cookbook room.

'We all turned up, one at a time. I don't remember who arrived first. We realised we didn't have enough chairs and people went looking for more. Despite the tension of the last few months, everyone was friendly enough when the meeting started. People chatted about what they'd been working on.

All the while, though, I could tell that something was up with Hailey. She looked about ready to explode.

'When it came to her turn, she told us she'd been given the contract, and editing of the novel had been scheduled. Hailey just kind of blurted it out. There was this stunned silence, and then people congratulated her. You could tell they were shocked, though.'

'You didn't like her book?' I said. '*The Second Death of Reginald Tanner*?'

'It wasn't so much that we didn't like it. The truth is that she barely wrote any of it. Everyone had given so much feedback over the years that we all felt like we owned the book. In her first draft, Hailey had Reginald Tanner dying halfway through! And the second half of the book was about someone else! Idiotic!' Piper shook her head. 'Anyway, I suppose that's why we were so outraged. She'd hardly had an original idea about the manuscript, and now she had a publishing deal. A *big* publishing deal.'

'Everyone was annoyed? Even Owen?'

Piper sighed. 'He didn't say much,' she said. 'Don't forget. He was in love with Hailey. But I think he was as shocked as everyone else. It seemed so unfair.'

'Piper,' I said carefully. 'I have to ask you about the incident with the book. The one in your bag.'

'That book.' Piper rolled her eyes. 'That was so awful. I

don't know how it got there, but I can make a guess. I've always thought it was Bella. She was weird. Vindictive. You can even see it in her books. They're a reflection of her.' She paused. 'And you know, other things happened. Someone vandalised Kylie's books at the library. Asher lost his keys. Jacob's car was damaged. Hailey's dog died. Something happened to everyone except Bella. It wouldn't have surprised me if she were behind it all.'

The front door opened, and a herd of teenagers bustled in.

Piper lowered her voice. 'I have to get back to work,' she said. 'Have you spoken to Bella yet?'

I shook my head.

'Then be careful,' Piper said. 'Nasty things happen when she's around.'

19

'This is not quite what I expected,' I said.

We were at the front gates of Bella Lodley's home. The property was a few kilometres inland from the coast, with a thick bush barrier running along the property line.

A driveway headed up to a distant house beyond, a modern-looking farmhouse with a wide verandah.

All this, Kim and I could see from my jeep at the end of the driveway. We couldn't see any further because of the gate barring our way.

'Bella's worth a few dollars,' Kim said, staring.

'It's not her money I'm interested in.' I nodded to the gate's intercom. 'I wonder if she'll let us in.'

'Only one way to find out.'

I leaned out the window and pushed the intercom.

'Yes?' a female voice answered after a brief pause.

'Bella Lodley?' I told her our names and that we wanted to speak to her about Plastic Apple.

'I'm not prepared for visitors.'

'I know that—'

'And I don't like being ambushed.'

'That's not my purpose.' I struggled to think of something to say. 'I understand you have a wonderful series of books you've been writing. We'd love to learn more about them, too.'

This was followed by a long silence. Then there was a final buzz of the gate and it slowly swung open.

Kim murmured under her breath. 'Flattery will get you everywhere.'

We drove up to the house.

The place was even more impressive close up with white timber and big windows and surrounded by low-lying shrubs. Extensive flower beds ran away from it like beams of light from a distant star.

Although I admired the setup, I doubted Bella did much of her own gardening. A man was mowing, and someone else digging the soil. Another man was trimming what looked like trees in an olive grove.

Good grief, I thought. *This woman is loaded.*

She didn't come out to greet us. I left Trixie in the car; I doubted this was a dog-friendly house. We climbed the steps to the verandah, pushed the doorbell, and waited. Almost a full minute passed before the door flew open.

'Yes?' the woman said.

Bella Lodley was eerily reminiscent of Gloria Swanson from Sunset Boulevard. She was older with too much makeup and a dress that could have been a nightie or an evening gown. Her hair was greying, and her face was drawn as if she spent her whole day scowling at people, which she probably did.

I wished I'd stayed in the car with Trixie.

'You'd like to know about my books?' Bella said.

'Your books,' I said, smiling brightly. 'And the Plastic Apple writing group.'

'That's been defunct for years.'

'I know.' We could stand here all day. 'It will only take a few minutes.'

The woman stared at us without blinking. 'You'd better come in,' she said. 'People should know the truth about that ghastly group.'

We followed her into a living room so large that it was embarrassing. The room had high ceilings, painfully white walls, and a gas fireplace. The coffee table was almost as big as a pool table, and the leather lounge surrounding it looked like it had never been sat on. A pile of crossword and word puzzle books sat on the table. This was obviously how Bella spent her spare time.

'Toxic,' Bella said after we sat down. 'That's how I would describe that group. Toxic.'

'There were problems with the other members?' I said.

Bella shrugged. 'Some were fine,' she said. 'And the venue was lovely. I simply love the smell of bookshops. And Ian's a charming man. You know his wife walked out on him? Quiet little thing. Hardly ever spoke to anyone and ran off to Queensland with a lover! Simply tragic. And she was an orphan with no family.' She shook her head. 'People are *so* ungrateful.'

'And the members of Plastic Apple?' I said, keen to get her back on track.

'Asher Vorback was a pleasant little man. Worked at the council for years. Something in the Building department.'

'Tenders and Procurement,' Kim corrected her.

Bella continued, unphased. 'He had his poetry,' she said. 'Basically a copy of the early Australian poets like Lawson and Patterson. Mind you, they understood rhythm and flow. Asher had no idea. Then there was Jacob. I suppose you'd think of him as the unofficial president of the club. Jacob's work was probably most similar to mine. He had an interest in family history. Mind you, his family weren't anyone you'd want to write about.'

'And the others?' I prompted.

'I suppose you'd refer to their work as *low-brow*.' Bella pulled a face. 'Kylie Crow and her ghastly romance books. Terrible. And she writes about ordinary folk. Who wants to read that rubbish? Readers want to know about people of influence.

People without influence are *not* interesting people.'

I don't think Bella and I will ever be friends.

Bella chuckled. It was like watching a witch laugh. 'Then we go from low-brow to bottom of the barrel,' she said. 'Owen had those terrible sword books he used to write. Piper was the same. Silly rot about dragons and elves. And Hailey—'

She stopped.

'You didn't like her work?' I said.

'A vampire novel.' Bella said the phrase as if Hailey had served up a plate of worms for an evening meal. 'I mean, really, it's the lowest trash. No one with any ability would write such a thing. And, to make matters worse, Hailey had no sense of style. No idea of plotting or characterisation. I helped her as much as I could. With my assistance, she turned an unreadable mess into a publishable book.'

'With the help of the others?' Kim prompted.

'I suppose so. Yes. They made some suggestions. But the most tiresome part was listening to the endless editing of the book. Constant. You can see why everyone was furious when she turned up saying she'd gotten a publishing deal—*and* was taking an overseas holiday. People exploded at the thought that she'd taken our suggestions and was about to profit from them.'

'Hailey apparently took her own life,' I pointed out. 'She suffered from anxiety.'

'*Ha!*' Bella snorted. 'I find that many young women these days are highly strung. They take drugs. Live the high life. No wonder they end up dying.'

'So her death…'

Bella shrugged. 'It could have been suicide,' she conceded. 'Or an accident. She fell from a cliff? That could happen to anyone.'

'And Owen?'

'He disappeared.'

If Bella had looked sour before, she now appeared downright vindictive. I wondered why momentarily and then was struck by the same idea I'd had about Piper. *Bella was in love with Owen.* Being an older woman made no difference. In the close quarters of the group, she'd fallen for Owen—hard—and her feelings were obviously not returned.

'Were Hailey and Owen close?' I asked.

'You realise they were in a relationship?'

'Really? Are you sure?'

'I saw them at the beach one day. They looked very chummy. I saw the look on his face. *Infatuated* with her, he was. He had poor taste, I suppose. Inexperience and youth go together. Owen killed himself after she died. That much, I'm sure of.'

I thought for a long moment. A lot of what Bella had said confirmed what the others had conveyed. There was still one other story I wanted to ask about.

'People have mentioned some strange incidents over those last few months,' I said. 'Almost as if the members were being targeted. Harassed.'

Bella shook her head. 'I don't know what you mean.'

I mentioned the stories we'd been told, and she shrugged.

'I remember my wonderful dog being attacked by that horrible mutt Hailey owned,' she said. 'Mona's since moved onto doggie heaven. I don't remember those other incidents. Anyway, I've prattled on long enough about that silly writers' group. Let me tell you about the Dankworths. I've got six books written in the series, and it's only a matter of time before they're picked up by a publisher.'

She regaled us with the adventures of her family saga and it was pretty much as Piper had described. It sounded like an episode of Dallas set in the Australian countryside. Everyone was sleeping with everyone else or wanting to murder them. Or both. I dutifully scribbled a few notes, but my mind was elsewhere.

Kim and I completed the interview.

As we got up to leave, I glanced over at Bella's bookcase. I couldn't help myself and arrowed over. 'Fantasy novels?' I said. The books were by various authors: J. R. R. Tolkien, Angus Beile, Ally Bolleed, Ursula Le Guin. 'I wouldn't think they'd be quite your style.'

Bella blushed. 'A guilty pleasure,' she said. 'Owen forced us to listen to his silly sword fighting books so often that he got me hooked.' She gave a short laugh. 'I suppose that's something I got from the meetings.'

We thanked her again and returned to my jeep.

'Goodness,' Kim said as she settled in beside me. 'What an unpleasant woman.'

'If there are aliens on Earth, she's definitely one of them.'

My phone rang. I didn't recognise the number.

'Rosie?' It was Barry Rycroft. 'Are you busy? I need to speak to you.'

'Right now?'

'It's urgent. Something's...happened.'

I promised I'd come to the hotel immediately. We left Bella's property. It was late afternoon now and the day was bright and clear. White cockatoos swept across the sky in a great sweeping arc as kangaroos watched us from roadside paddocks.

'What did you make of what Bella said?' Kim asked.

'I've got a gut feeling about something.' I told her about my suspicions regarding Bella and Owen. 'Love makes people do crazy things. Bella was an older woman. That doesn't mean she couldn't be in love with him. And Piper loved Owen, too.'

Kim frowned, thinking. 'Hailey and Owen could have been murdered out of jealousy,' she said. 'First, Hailey, because she was the object of Owen's affection. Then one of the women could have killed Owen because he rejected them.'

'True.' I was feeling gloomy and I told Kim why. 'Let's not forget that someone got Hailey up that cliff and pushed—or threw—her over. Would Bella or Piper be able to entice her up there? Maybe. They certainly wouldn't be able to carry Hailey, although you know who could?'

'Owen,' Kim sighed.

'Bingo. And that takes us back to our original theory. The one that's bounced around for years: Hailey rejected Owen, and he killed her in a fit of temper. Overcome with grief, he finally took his own life.' I paused. 'And you know the logical place where that would have happened?'

Kim groaned. 'Not Elk's Gap?' she said. 'Don't say we have to head back there. Where would we even start?'

'You remember that object at the base of the cliff?'

'That could have been anything. Junk or a scrap of clothing. It doesn't mean that Owen did a swan dive off the top.'

'But it doesn't mean he didn't either,' I told her. 'His body could have been at the bottom of that cliff for years.'

'So we're going bushwalking?'

'We are, though not right now. Now, we will find out what's got Barry in a tizz.'

We reached Cape Carson and made our way to the hotel, where we found Barry sitting in the bar, moodily gazing out at the ocean.

'Girls,' he said. 'Thanks for coming so quickly.'

'What is it?' I asked.

'It's the relic,' he said, lowering his voice. 'I've received a ransom note!'

20

'Really?' I said. 'Let me see it.'

He handed the note to me. It was typed and printed on plain white paper. It read:

It will cost you fifty thousand for the return of the relic. If you contact the police, you'll never see it again. Instructions will follow.

'Fifty thousand dollars?' Kim said. 'That's a lot of money.'

'But we've got to get it back,' Barry said. 'It's priceless.'

I wasn't so sure about that. The Mona Lisa was supposed to be priceless, and I thought it was a lovely painting of a woman with an odd smile. As far as the relic went, it looked like junk to me. And definitely not junk that had fallen off a flying saucer.

'You need to go to the police,' I said.

Barry shook his head. 'The note specifically says *not* to contact the police.' He gazed at the page. 'This is all my fault. I should have stored the relic in a hotel safe. Then it would have been okay.'

I didn't know what to say. I wanted to sympathise with Barry, yet I thought he was upset over nothing. What I did do was bring him up to date on what had happened in the house on Crescent Drive.

'So you came close to retrieving it,' Barry said, brightening. 'Although you must have spooked the criminal. I'm surprised they didn't leave town.'

'He has fifty thousand reasons not to,' Kim said.

'But that's chicken feed compared to what the relic would fetch on the black market. A collector would pay millions.'

'So why doesn't he do that?' I asked.

'He's after quick cash. The extortionist can make his money and be gone in days as opposed to months or years.'

'So you'll pay the ransom?'

'We don't have any other choice.'

'Where will you get the money?'

Barry swallowed. 'I don't have that kind of cash,' he said. 'Fortunately, AFSA has had several generous donations over the years. We have more than enough to cover that.' He bit his lip. 'I'll have to put it to the committee: Neo and Jasper. They won't be happy, but there's nothing else we can do.'

'Do you think they'll approve it?'

'I don't know. I hope so.'

Considering he'd accused Jasper of stealing the relic, I could only imagine the frosty reception he'd face. We wished Barry good luck, and I asked him to keep us posted. Kim and I left. We both had to return to work. Saying I'd catch up with her later, I went back to the office.

Harry yelled out as Trixie and I bustled in the front door. 'Is that Rosie Ryan?' he called. 'You still work here?'

'I'm hot on the trail of two stories.'

He asked me to bring him up to date with what I'd been investigating. At the end, he shook his head sadly. 'I'm so sorry,' he said. 'I had no idea that sending you to that kooky UFO conference would cause so much drama. You say this fellow Barry will pay the ransom?'

'As long as the committee approves it.'

'I imagine they will. There can't be too many UFO spare parts around. So Hailey had a publishing deal? And Owen also had interest from the same company?'

'Lancelot Press. They're in Ballarat.'

'Sounds like they'd be worth a visit.'

I agreed. Heading to my desk, I found Jay sitting miserably at his computer. 'Rosie,' he said. 'I can't take this any longer!'

'What's wrong?'

'It's hanging out with all the old ladies. I'll go mad if I have to hear about Shirley Wilson's lumbago one more time. And Bernice Pillar is as deaf as a post. She keeps calling me Kaye!'

Laughing, I told him to focus on the positive. 'They're a lovely bunch of ladies,' I said. 'My grandmother's one of them.'

'I know. But there's so much lavender!'

'You'll survive!'

After bringing my notes up to date, I found the details online for Lancelot Press and rang them. After speaking to a secretary, I was put through to the owner, a man named Bly Simmons.

'Hailey Lawrence?' Bly said. 'I remember her. The woman who killed herself?'

'I'm doing a retrospective on her death and was wondering if I could come in and chat.'

He agreed to a meeting that afternoon. Hanging up, I glanced at my watch. I had just enough time to grab a coffee. Trixie and I went to my jeep and, a few minutes later, were at the counter at Sandy's.

As Sandy steamed the milk, I turned around to see George enter. 'Hey Rosie,' he said. 'More caffeine?'

'Can't survive without it.' I paused. 'Nice dinner the other evening.'

'Yeah. Adrian's a good guy.' George ordered his coffee. 'You and Todd seem to be getting on.'

Hmm, I thought. *I wonder where this is leading.*

'You and Sadie too,' I said. 'Although Todd and I are just friends.'

We paid for our coffees and headed outside.

'I'm sorry about what happened with Nico,' I said.

George didn't speak for a moment. 'Nico brought all that on himself,' he said, finally. 'You never should have been caught up in it.' He struggled to speak for a moment. 'I'm sorry about everything that happened between...me and Blossom.'

Years before, walking in on George and his former girlfriend, Blossom, had ended our marriage. That was a long time ago. He was with Sadie now and I—well—was still single. Which I didn't mind.

'You've apologised before,' I said. 'There was something wrong with our marriage. I don't know what. Maybe our relationship had run its course. People change.'

'Neither of us are the people we were twenty-five years ago.'

'At least we got a beautiful daughter out of it.'

George smiled, and for a moment, it was like looking at the man I'd met all those years ago. And a different one, too. He was older and maybe more mature too. I wished him a good day, retrieved Trixie from her place on the footpath, and headed to my jeep. Soon I was on my way to Ballarat. Mother Nature had turned on the weather for us. The day was clear, and the breeze that blew in from the west was mild and warm.

We passed stands of bush and huge sweeping fields filled with canola crops. The bright yellow flowers were stunning at this time of year. Windmills turned lazily on the horizon. As I came over a hill, I glimpsed a hawk, hundreds of feet up, lazily coasting on the wind.

'It's a beautiful day,' I told Trixie.

She let out a satisfied pant in agreement.

The journey to Ballarat was about two hours. I took the road north to Darlington and then northwest through Wallinduc and Pitfield. I'd visited the outback a few times and was struck by how unending the horizon could be in all directions. It was similar here, too, although the hills here were green and fertile.

'There's a lot of country out here,' I told Trixie.

Less impressed than me, she settled down for a snooze.

Arriving in Ballarat just after two, I drove through the old city, passing massive granite and sandstone buildings built during the 1860s gold rush. The streets were broad, with footpaths shaded by awnings and old eucalypts decorating the streetscape. This was one of Victoria's most beautiful regional cities, and I always enjoyed coming here.

It only took a few minutes to navigate through town to Lake Wendouree. The lake was one of the area's highlights, a vast body of water with a six-kilometre circumference. Although this would have been the perfect day to stroll around the lake, I had work to do. Casting a regretful eye at the glistening water, I drove on, stopping in front of an old art deco building. After winding down the window so Trixie could get some air, I headed inside.

A woman manned the front desk. Behind her, a maze of

smaller offices was visible through another doorway.

The owner's office led off reception, and clearly had the best view, with glimpses of the nearby lake. The receptionist pointed me in.

Bly Simmons was surprisingly young. No more than thirty. He had swept back red hair and, incongruously, wore a tweed suit and a bowtie.

'Ah-ha,' he said. 'Rosie Ryan.'

'Thanks for making some time.'

We shook hands and I sat. As expected, while one wall was dominated by a big window with a view, the other three were lined with bookshelves. These were obviously books the firm had published over the years. Bly gave me a gentle smile. 'You've got some questions about Hailey Lawrence? A terrible loss. Losing a promising young writer like her at such a young age.'

'She was obviously talented.'

'Absolutely. Would have had a successful career, I imagine. I looked up the correspondence before you arrived.' He referred to his screen. 'Her book was *The Second Death of Reginald Tanner*. A vampire novel, I seem to recall.'

'That's it.'

'I remember reading it when it arrived. Had a lot of promise.'

'You decided not to publish it?'

Bly shook his head. 'The book goes through rounds of editing,' he explained. 'It's a long road to publication and virtually impossible if the author's not around.'

'How successful do you think it would have been?'

'It's impossible to say,' Bly said. 'As publishers, we do what we can to promote a book, but luck is always a component. Although vampire novels seem like a safe bet, they're a trend that comes and goes like the tide.'

I nodded. 'What do you recall about Hailey?'

'Not much, to be honest,' Bly said apologetically. 'It was a long time ago, and I see a lot of authors. I recall she was quiet. Listened a lot. Didn't say much. She was happy with what we were offering.'

'Can you tell me how much that was?'

'Unfortunately, not. We can't share contractual details, even if the contracts didn't proceed to fruition.'

'It seemed unusual to those who knew her that she'd kill herself after receiving such good news. Hailey was also planning a holiday to Europe.'

'I see.' Bly shook his head. 'An absolute tragedy. I seem to recall...'

'Yes?'

'There was something about her death not being a suicide. Her sister rang me about it?'

'There was talk about a young man being obsessed with her,'

I said. 'Possibly disguising her murder as suicide.' I continued. 'Did you remember Hailey mentioning her writers' group? Plastic Apple?'

Bly frowned. 'Vaguely. She said they'd been helpful.'

'You know that Owen Stamett was also a member?'

'I don't know that name.'

'You were interested in seeing his books. A series of fantasy novels. You had some interest in publishing them.'

'Really? And what happened?'

'He died a month after Hailey.'

'Owen Stamett?' Bly checked his computer. When he found nothing, he asked his receptionist to check her files. They had no record of Owen or his publishing deal. 'Are you certain it was us?'

'I'm sure. Wait a minute. I took a photo of the letter you sent.' I showed him the picture. 'Do you remember this?'

Bly took a long time to examine the image. 'This is odd,' he said grimly. 'That's our logo, and that's my name, but it's not my signature. It's not even close. And frankly, we don't send letters out to clients. We ring or email them.'

I stared at the picture on my phone in confusion. 'And Owen's books?' I said, my eyes angling up. 'The first was called *The Cry of Kaled's Sword*. You don't know it?'

Bly slowly shook his head. 'I've never heard of it,' he said. 'We don't publish a lot of fantasy, anyway.'

'Thanks,' I said. 'You've been helpful.'

And I meant it, although I had no idea what any of this meant.

21

'Now that's weird,' Kim said.

We were sitting in the front window of Sandy's. It was early evening, and the bay was calm. Inside, the diner was busy with customers, while locals enjoying the spring warmth strolled down the footpath outside.

I was forgoing food in exchange for another coffee. At least it was medium-sized. A jumbo-sized shot of caffeine would have rocketed me to the moon and back.

'You're telling me,' I said. 'On one hand, we've got a letter saying the publisher was interested in Owen's novels. On the other hand, the publisher knew nothing about it.'

'The publisher—what's this guy's name—Bly Simmons could be lying,' Kim suggested. 'Maybe he kept them for himself to publish.'

I considered this. 'That's possible,' I admitted. 'Though, it's a big risk. And publishers generally don't need to steal a writer's work. There's always plenty of books in the pipeline.'

'Could Owen have been trying to impress Hailey?'

'Hailey was already dead by then.' I rubbed my chin. 'The letter could have been a callous joke.'

'People have described Bella as nasty. Could she have done it?'

'It's a cruel joke if she did.'

'And let's not forget that Owen's books have disappeared.'

I nodded. 'There could be numerous explanations for that: Owen could have destroyed them in a fit of anger, taken them with him—wherever he went—or someone stole them after his death.' I thought for a moment. 'You know what this means?'

'That we should give up on this whole thing because it's too difficult?'

'No. We need to return to Elk's Gap and search that valley.'

Kim stared at me as if I'd lost my mind. 'Are you kidding?' she asked. 'You saw how dense that bushland is. You could search for years and not find anything.'

'True. But I've got a secret weapon.'

'Really? You've got a superpower I don't know about?'

The next day, we returned to the Kilkenny Arms, where we found Jasper Kidwell sitting forlornly at the bar.

'Jasper?' I said.

He turned. 'Hey girls. This is a nice surprise. I wanted to talk to you about this extortion demand.'

'Great. We need to speak to you as well.'

Kim and I bought soft drinks and joined him in a corner where we could talk in peace.

'We're not happy about this ransom,' Jasper said. 'It's a lot of money to pay out.'

'Has the association got that much?' I asked.

'Enough—and more. We've had a lot of generous donations over the years. They were never intended to be used like this, though I can't see a way around it. The relic belongs to AFSA, and it's one of the only pieces of a flying saucer on the planet.' He paused. 'Barry and I aren't exactly talking. It's a shame because we've been friends for years. I know he regrets what happened. When we get the relic back—if we get it back—he's agreed to step down as president.'

'Who will take over the job?' Kim asked.

'Probably me. Once the relic's returned, we'll store it in a secure facility where the members can view it at any time.'

'Jasper,' Kim said patiently. 'How can you be sure it's real? The relic could be a fake.'

He shook his head. 'It looks the same as the picture from the Blackwood encounter. And Barry had it tested years ago. It's an aluminium alloy, light and durable. Exactly the material you'd want for spaceflight.'

It was pointless trying to talk sense to Jasper. He was too far down the conspiracy rabbit hole. 'There's something else I'd like to speak to you about,' I said, and explained about Owen going missing in the Elk's Gap valley three years before. 'Kim and I spotted something from the clifftop. It could be anything though we think it's worth checking out. The problem is—'

'—getting to it?'

'That's it.'

Jasper chuckled. 'People don't realise how dense the bush can be until they start traipsing about in it. Then they find it can be both beautiful and deadly.' He scrutinised us. 'You think it's easier and safer to access the site with a drone?'

I nodded. 'I remember you saying you'd worked with drones a lot.'

'Barry has too. We often fly our drones on weekends.' His face clouded over. 'At least, we used to. I hope we can put this whole thing behind us and return to how things were.'

I nodded sympathetically. Seeing how unhappy Jasper looked made me realise how painful this incident must have been for him and the other members. Although their beliefs were kooky, the organisation gave them a community. A lot of their closest friends were probably in AFSA.

Jasper continued. 'I have a drone I can lend you,' he said. 'It's basic, but it'll do the job.'

'Is it difficult to operate?' Kim asked.

'Not at all. There's an app you can download to your phone. I'll send you the link.'

Within minutes, we had the software installed and Jasper had taken us to his room, where he produced the drone. It was square-shaped, little bigger than a football, with a camera below and propellers at each corner.

'We'll head out onto the beach,' he said. 'I'll give you some training.'

We collected Trixie from the footpath and ten minutes later were on the beach with Jasper showing us the basic operations. 'This takes you up,' he explained, indicating one of the buttons on the app. 'And this is down. Left, right, back, and forth are the four arrows on the screen, like a compass. When you're in the bush, the most difficult thing is avoiding the trees. This is worth money, so you don't want to lose it. If you do, I need you to buy me a replacement.'

Both Kim and I tried out the device. Although we were both shaky at first, it didn't take long to master. The trick was to take everything slowly; rapid movements produced inconsistent results.

'There are several automatic functions,' he explained after we'd brought it into land. 'Most, like waypoint flying, you won't need. However, you can configure the device to cover a search grid, which can be handy. You'll probably use the hover control, too.'

'This is really helpful,' I said as Jasper handed us the device. 'How can we repay you?'

'No need. You're a true believer like the rest of us, Rosie.' Jasper winked. 'You're one of us.'

'Er, yes.'

We thanked Jasper again and returned to my car. Trixie had been fascinated by the drone the whole time we were on the beach. Now she eyed it warily as she sat beside it on the back seat.

'It's fine, Trixie,' I said. 'That drone is our friend.'

She tilted her head, and Kim laughed. 'I don't think she believes you.'

We drove out of town to Elk's Gap. It was lunchtime now, and I wished we'd stopped for a meal. Strangely, it seemed, coffee alone wasn't enough to sustain a person.

After getting out of the jeep, I set the drone on the ground. Kim had shown more expertise with the app than me, so I got her to take control. Within minutes, she had the flying device coasting slowly over the treetops. Watching the screen, I saw the landscape edging by. 'Don't go too fast,' I advised. 'No...that's too slow...just a bit quicker...'

'Rosie,' she muttered, focusing on her screen. 'I have this all under control.'

I stayed quiet.

She aimed the device at the cliff face from where we'd seen the flash of red. Then she swung the drone around and gradually descended. There was no sign of the item we'd glimpsed from above.

'I can't see it,' Kim said, peering at the screen.

'Me neither.'

She slowed the drone to a crawl, and a patch of earth and grass appeared in the undergrowth. I asked Kim to set the device to hover.

'Is that what I think it is?' she asked.

'An old trail?'

'Looks like it.'

I asked Kim to adjust the height of the drone, and she raised it about fifty feet. *There it is.* The device was a black dot hovering over the trees. We walked down the road, finally stopping at an indentation in the undergrowth. Beyond the thick shrubs facing the road was an old trail winding away into the bush.

'This could have been a fire trail,' Kim said.

'Once, maybe.' I peered into the undergrowth. It was easy to see why we hadn't spotted it before. It was now mostly gorse and weeds. 'This hasn't been used in years.'

Kim peered through the trees. 'I think the drone's hovering at the other end,' she said.

'Then that's where we have to go.'

After traipsing over the shrubs, we started up the uneven trail. It was so overgrown that it was impossible to see what lay ahead. I kept Trixie close as we pushed through patches of the spiny shrub. Although it was early spring, there could still be snakes out here. At least, if you didn't disturb them, they mostly left you alone.

About fifteen minutes later, feeling hot, sticky, and covered in scratches, we reached a spot where the drone hovered high overhead. Kim carefully manoeuvred it down through the tree canopy, and it came to an untidy landing in a nearby grevillea.

'Rosie,' Kim began as she dragged it free. 'When we go out next time, can we do the movies instead? This is like a death march.'

'Next time, it's popcorn and ice cream all the way. I promise.' I grabbed Kim's arm. 'Look,' I said, pointing. 'Over there.'

A flash of red lay in the bush about twenty metres away. We stamped along the trail, pushing aside weeds as we went. Finally, the object that I'd spotted came into view.

'You've got to be kidding,' I said.

'An old soft drink can.'

I picked it up feeling deflated. We'd come all this way for nothing! I examined the can more closely. 'You know, this isn't that old. Only a few years.'

'You think Owen could have left it?'

'I don't know.'

We continued down the rough trail.

My eyes swept the undergrowth, but nothing seemed out of the ordinary. The bush could be like this sometimes: a mesh of woven bushes and shrubs that blended into a tapestry of colour. We continued on for another fifty metres before the rocky trail came unceremoniously to an end.

'Oh dear,' I said. 'This is it.'

Kim peered up through the trees. 'There's the lookout up there.'

I sighed. We'd come a long way for seemingly no reason. I was tired and hot and had torn my shirt. I was also thirsty. We'd forgotten to bring water, a rookie mistake. As I turned to leave, my gaze caught sight of a vine—and I stared. *That's no vine.* Grabbing Kim's arm, I drew her after me.

The vine was a rope stretched over a mottled brown and green camouflage tarp. I scanned the shape underneath. 'That's a car,' I breathed.

'Do you think—'

'I don't know what to think.'

I pulled the rope free and dragged up the end of the tarp. The car underneath was an old bush green Ford Focus. It had been parked nose-first under the trees. We pulled the tarp clear. The vehicle had been here for years. Three years, at a guess. 'Owen owned a Ford Focus,' I said. 'I remember seeing it in a picture at his home. This must be his car.'

'So he dumped it here before going on the run?' Kim said. 'A perfectly good car?'

'I don't know.'

The tyres were flat, and the car had sunk into the under-growth. Despite being protected by the tarp, the duco had started to crack. Miraculously, a vine had grown up through the car and filled much of the interior. I pushed through shrubs to the driver's side door. With effort, I was able to wrench it open, the hinges giving a nerve-jarring squeal.

The glove box contained an old road map, a few receipts, and a packet of jelly beans, melted into a misshapen lump. I checked the middle storage compartment and found a small bag of coins and some scraps of paper. Although they were faded, I could make out a few words.

'Lazarus sword...battle of Bremni...' I stopped. 'These must be notes for Owen's book. This is his car.'

Kim was still at the rear. 'Rosie,' she called. 'Unlock the boot, and I'll take a look inside.'

I found the boot release lever and heard a dull click as it opened. 'Looks like Owen abandoned his car here,' I said. 'He must have had another vehicle waiting. Or he hitchhiked.'

'I don't think so.'

'What do you mean?' I asked as I rounded the vehicle. She was peering into the boot. 'Do you think—'

I stared down in horror.

What lay in the boot had once been a man. That much I could tell from his clothing. His t-shirt and jeans were bloodied and stuck to the bones beneath. The corpse had been here for years. Staring up at us was his skull and in the middle of the forehead was a small hole. A bullet wound.

'You're right,' I said. 'Owen didn't go anywhere.'

22

'Okay,' Todd said, crossing the road to my jeep. 'It's official. That's Owen Stamett's car. I'd be willing to bet it's his body too, but we'll have to wait for a post-mortem to be sure.'

Two hours had passed since Kim and I had discovered the body. Since then, the tiny stretch of quiet road had become a hive of activity as police, personnel from Parks and Wildlife, and a forensics team combed the area. Hovering overhead was a helicopter searching for more evidence.

Kim and I had sat in my car all this time waiting. Trixie had fallen asleep. Even I felt like nodding off. I leaned out the window. 'So the deaths of Owen and Hailey must be linked,' I said.

Todd hesitated. 'It's too early to say for sure,' he said. 'Hailey died a month before him. And her death was ruled a suicide.'

'Come on,' I groaned. 'Two members of Plastic Apple were killed within a month, and you think it's a coincidence?'

Kim chimed in. 'Maybe Owen murdered Hailey,' she said.

'And someone found out and took revenge.'

'That's possible,' Todd agreed. 'Any evidence?'

'Must you always insist on evidence?' I asked.

'It's kind of my job.'

'Spoilsport.'

Todd said he'd let us know if he discovered anything. We left and drove back to town. Kim and I quickly threw down a meal of burgers and chips before I dropped her at the library. I was about to continue to the office when my phone rang: Barry.

'Rosie?' he said. 'Are you able to come to the hotel?'

'Is it urgent?'

'Something's come up about the ransom.'

Ten minutes later, I was hurrying through the lobby of the Kilkenny Arms, where I found Barry, Jasper, and Neo waiting grim-faced.

'What is it?' I asked.

'Not out here,' Barry said.

No one said anything until we had gone upstairs to the meeting room and settled around the conference table. Barry removed a letter from his pocket, slid it across to me, and I read:

You'll deliver the fifty thousand tonight at 10.00pm. The money must be in small denomination bills. If you don't comply, I will sell the relic on the black market, and you'll never see it again.

But it was the next part that made my jaw drop.

The exchange will happen at the Old Huxley Bridge outside of Barkly. I want Rosie Ryan to bring the cash. She will wait in the middle of the bridge. If she doesn't come alone—if I smell a trap—you'll never see the relic again. Do not involve the police.

'Me?' I squeaked. 'They want me?'

'Looks that way,' Neo said thoughtfully. 'I'd say this rules out my theory that the relic was stolen by the CIA. This isn't their style at all. It could be ex-KGB who have fallen on hard times—'

'Anyway,' Barry said. 'It looks like we now have a good chance of getting the relic back.'

'Our *only* chance,' Jasper added. 'But it means you'll have to go alone.'

I stared at them. 'Look,' I said. 'I'm sorry, but I can't get involved in delivering ransom money. It's not part of my job description. I'm a journalist, not a commando.'

'But you have to go,' Neo said. 'The ransom note says it must be you.'

Barry nodded. 'They may not hand over the relic if someone else turns up.'

'This is a matter for the police,' I said firmly.

'The note specifically says not to involve the police,' Jasper pointed out. 'We may never see the relic again if we tell the cops.'

'And I must point out,' Barry added, 'that the relic is priceless. I don't like paying a criminal money for something that belongs to us. But we have no other choice.'

I stared at them helplessly. 'The criminal might be armed,' I said. 'This could be dangerous.'

'I have some weapons you can take,' Neo said. 'Homemade explosives and a replica gun I made from spare parts. The trigger's iffy, though, so don't point it at yourself in case—'

'I'm not taking a gun. Or explosives. Or—'

'—and I've got some homemade stun grenades—'

While Neo detailed how I could become a one-woman SWAT team, I readied myself to say *no*.

That would have been the sensible answer. A short, sharp *no* followed by me marching off and storming into Harry's office. Then I would yell at him for half an hour before sitting down and having a huge cry.

And I knew what was stopping me from doing that: *guilt*. I'd destroyed the universe. Well, not the entire universe, just a large-scale structure that represented a big chunk of it, but it was enough. It represented the work of a bunch of volunteers squirreling away till the early morning hours for over a year. The model of Laniakea had been beautiful, and I'd destroyed it.

The least I could do was make amends.

'Okay,' I cut Neo short. 'I'll do it, though I'm not taking any weapons. Knowing my luck, I'd blow myself up or shoot myself in the foot.'

'It's easy to do,' Neo said. 'I lost a little toe to a crossbow.'

'We've got the cash,' Jasper explained. 'It was easy to arrange, although it involved channelling money through Liechtenstein and Kiribati.'

'Oh great,' I said weakly.

Barry nodded to a duffle bag under the table. 'It goes without saying that this mustn't leave your sight,' he said. 'You must only hand over the money in exchange for the relic.'

'Yes,' Jasper agreed. 'Don't be heroic. Don't do anything foolish.'

It was too late to avoid doing anything foolish. 'I won't,' I promised. Adventure mode had been far more fun. Now the narrative had switched to something out of a spy thriller; joy had been replaced by a cold sense of foreboding.

Jasper reached into his pocket and produced what looked like old-style Nokia phones. 'These are handy little devices of my own design,' he said. 'They piggyback off the Telstra network and will allow us to stay in contact.'

'I already have a phone,' I said.

Neo leaned close. 'Authorities can listen in,' she said. 'We need to stay off the grid.'

'Great.'

'We'll need code names for this operation. We'll be Larry, Moe, and Curly Joe, and you can be Charlie.'

'Charlie?'

'Charlie Chaplin.'

Jasper looked disappointed. 'Can't we do the James Bond actors instead?'

'Which ones?' Barry asked.

'Only the best: Sean Connery, Roger Moore, and Daniel Craig.'

'What about George Lazenby?' Neo asked, thinking. 'He was Australian.'

'He was always my favourite,' Jasper said, 'despite only being in one film.'

After several more minutes of arguing, it was decided that Neo would be Sean, Barry would take on the role of Daniel, leaving Jasper to assume George's identity. That left me to be Roger.

'Are you sure this is necessary?' I asked. 'Doesn't it all seem a little too...cloak and dagger?'

'The walls have ears,' Barry informed me. 'Noises have been coming from my attic for months. The pest controller says it's a possum, but I think it may be ASIO.'

Jasper continued. 'Now, I suggest you head home and get some rest. We'll be in contact later to check-in. Remember, don't let the bag out of your sight and only exchange it for the relic.'

I went home with Trixie and the bag on the passenger seat

beside me. Once I got there, I was relieved to see that Nan hadn't returned. I tucked the bag under my bed and rang Kim to give her the news.

'Are you insane?' were her first words after I told her what I had planned for the night. 'You've got to go to the police!'

'I can't, Kim. Barry and the others might never see their relic...thingy again.'

'Bad luck! It's too dangerous.'

'But I broke their universe!'

'It was a Lego universe! They'll get over it! You can't do this!'

'I've got to.'

Kim groaned. 'Okay, but I'm coming with you.'

'The extortionist said to go alone.'

'Of course, they did! They always do! Rosie, it's far too dangerous to go alone. At least take me. I'll stay in the car. With any luck, I'll be able to help in case there's trouble.'

Having Kim there would make me feel safer. It was better to have some backup than none at all. 'All right,' I said reluctantly. 'Do you know you're the best friend in the world?'

'I know. Now, enough with the mushy stuff. We need to plan.'

A few hours later, I picked Kim up from her place, and we headed out of town toward Barkly. By then, the countryside was dark and clear and moonless. My heart was thudding, and I felt a little light-headed.

I can't believe I'm doing this, I thought. *I'm quitting the next time Harry volunteers me for some crackpot assignment!*

Barkly came up all too soon. We drove through the town, continuing to the west. The Huxley Bridge was part of the old train line, discontinued in the sixties. The bridge was a big sturdy thing made of granite that traversed a fifty-metre deep ravine.

I pulled over in the shadows of a tree beside a pile of rotting sleepers. I'd been here during the day. The rail line, rusting and overgrown with weeds, cut through the countryside to the bridge, although there was little to see at this time of night. The hills around were an undulating carpet, lit only by starlight.

'Are we there yet?' Kim hissed from her hiding place on the floor behind me.

'We sure are.'

The discordant tones of a nursery rhyme exploded like a bomb in the night.

'Good grief,' I muttered, pulling out the phone Jasper had given me.

'Is that *Mary had a Little Lamb*?' Kim whispered.

'Yes.' I answered it. 'Jasper?'

'It's me, uh, George. Roger.'

I waited. 'Yes, George.'

'You have to identify yourself as Roger and sign off with Roger to indicate the message is received and understood.

Roger.'

'Oh. Right. Well, I'm Roger. Roger.' I paused and decided I wanted to continue. I glanced at my watch. 'I'm in position. It's five minutes to ten, and I'm about to leave the car.' No one replied. Then I remembered. 'Roger?'

'Okay, Roger,' Neo said. 'Understood. Are you alone, Roger? Roger.'

I cast a careful glance back at Kim. 'I am alone, Roger. I mean Neo...George...Mary. Anyway, I'm leaving now. I'll let you know what happens. Roger, Roger. Um, bye.'

I hung up.

'Well.' Kim's voice came from the back. 'That was as clear as mud.'

'Compared to that conversation, handing over ransom money in exchange for an alien relic should be easy.' It was time to leave. 'Stay here and don't let yourself be seen. I'll be back soon. Hopefully.'

'Be careful.'

The air was frigid and still as I climbed from the vehicle.

What am I doing? This is insane! So what if I destroyed the universe! Accidents happen!!

Gravel crunched underfoot as I headed for the bridge. My hand was gripping the duffle bag like a talon. I'd never carried so much money in my life. These days, in an era of card usage, cash was a rarity. Now I had enough on me for a down payment on a house.

Don't mess this up.

My eyes were growing accustomed to the dark. I could make out details in the landscape: silhouetted trees, a fence line disappearing over a hill, a disused railcar, the dark ravine below. I stopped, listened, and heard jangling water. It had to be the narrow creek that ran through the gorge. The only other sound was my jeep's engine ticking intermittently in the night.

The bridge was a hundred metres across with a metre-high retaining wall. At least there was little chance of me tumbling over the edge. I continued scanning the darkness. There was no sign of the extortionist. He could be on the other side of the bridge, or I could have already passed him in the dark.

I'm being watched.

Someone's eyes were on me. The barrier wall on one side of the bridge lay in more darkness than the other. *He could be hiding in the shadows.* I stopped momentarily and listened.

Nothing.

Thank goodness Kim is here, I thought. My heart was pounding so hard I felt lightheaded.

Bing!

The sound of a message arriving split the night. It was like a tiny explosion. With my free hand, I read my phone:

Drop the bag over the side

'What?' I muttered.

Gripping the cold barrier wall, I peered over the edge and into the ravine. At first, I saw nothing. Just patches of ebony black.

Then I made out more detail. A clump of trees. Scattered boulders. Reeds growing in the shallow stream. A light flickered in the gloom.

That's someone's phone, I realised.

'Where's the relic?' I called.

My voice sounded thin in the cold night.

They tapped on their phone.

Bing!

I read:

Drop the bag over, and you can have the relic

'Not until you give me proof that you've got it!' I yelled.

The light on the extortionist's phone came to life, and I saw a figure in black wearing a balaclava. This was the same person I'd seen at the house on Crescent Drive. A cold shiver jangled my spine. This person had assaulted and tied me to a chair. My fear coalesced into a heady lump of rage. I felt like going down there, snatching up a rock, and whacking them.

The extortionist pointed to his feet, indicating an open canvas bag. Inside lay the silver relic.

Okay, I thought. *At least he's brought it with him.*

Which meant I faced an awful dilemma. I had to trust that this person would take the money and leave the relic. Although maybe there was a way I could buy some time.

'Okay,' I called. 'Catch!'

I tossed the bag of money over the edge, aiming it for a spot on the other side of the narrow creek. It landed in weedy grass with a dull thud. Simultaneously I activated the torch on my phone as I raced back along the length of the bridge.

'Kim!' I screamed.

Without waiting for her, I rounded the end of the bridge and started down the uneven slope, the light on my phone dancing crazily in the darkness. It was slow going. I wasn't so interested in catching the criminal as I was in retrieving the relic. The sound of the extortionist's feet splashing in water echoed about the ravine, then: the scrape of the duffle bag, footsteps, an engine roaring to life.

A motorcycle!

My foot caught on a rock, and I went tumbling. I desperately grabbed for weeds to slow my fall. My ankle hit another rock, and pain shot up my leg. I somehow struggled to my feet again, my phone still in hand as I continued to the creek. The motorcyclist snapped his headlight on. He had the duffle bag attached to his back as he took off, the bike bouncing over uneven rocks as he charged up the creek.

I staggered over to the bag containing the relic. 'Thank goodness,' I muttered. The relic was still inside. I didn't touch it. I'd told Barry and the others that I would retrieve the relic.

What I hadn't told them was what I intended to do next: take it to the police to be fingerprinted.

Kim joined me. 'Are you all right?'

'I'm okay. Kind of.'

'Should we go after him?'

The criminal zoomed up a shallow section of the ravine to the top and disappeared from view.

'No,' I sighed. 'We got what we came for.'

23

It was late as I limped into the foyer of the Kilkenny Arms, where Barry, Jasper, and Neo were sitting at a table. The trio was gloomily nursing their drinks. I could understand their concern. I'd turned off the phone Jasper had given me and ignored their calls on my regular mobile.

Neo glanced up, and she yelled. Then her eyes angled down to my empty hands.

'It's fine,' I assured them. 'The exchange happened, and the relic is safe.'

'Great,' Barry said. 'So where is it?'

This would be the more difficult part. 'It's with the police,' I said, and before they could protest, I continued. 'It needs to be fingerprinted. Both it and the bag need to be checked. If there are any clues as to the identity of whoever pulled this heist, the police will find them.'

Neo's face darkened. 'But they're the cops,' she said. 'You know they can't be trusted.'

'Neo,' I said. 'This is my town, and I know the local cops. They're a good bunch, and I'm sure they'll do the right thing.'

Jasper looked uncertain but grudgingly nodded. 'Then we need to be grateful for what you've done,' he said. 'Are you limping?'

'It's a long story.' I wasn't going into detail about what happened at the bridge. 'It's not important. But I've had a long day, and I need to sleep. I've got Kim waiting in the car.'

The three thanked me, although it wasn't with wholesale enthusiasm. I could understand their reticence.

They saw police, governments, big business—in fact, anyone in an official position of power—to be part of a global conspiracy. I promised I'd catch up with them. Then I returned to my jeep, dropped Kim at her place, and went home.

Nan and her boyfriend Dave were curled up on the couch. He'd fallen asleep while Nan sat and knitted. She glanced up as Trixie came bounding over.

'What happened to you?' Nan asked.

'Just the usual.'

'You didn't knock over the universe again?'

'No. And it's too much to go into. I'm off to bed.'

'Not before you grab yourself an icepack.'

It was a good idea. I'd suffered so many injuries that we now kept a medical pack in the freezer. After wrapping it around my ankle, I headed to my bedroom. The tiredness was starting to come on now. I lay back on the bed and was about to put out the light when my phone rang.

Who—?

'Todd?' I said.

'Rosie,' he said. 'I wanted to check on how you're doing.'

He'd been all business at the police station, and I could see had been struggling to not chastise me. I imagined he was about to open the floodgates. 'Well,' I said. 'My ankle is aching like crazy, and I feel like death.'

'You're lucky to be alive,' Todd said. 'You know doing that exchange with the extortionist was probably the most stupid thing you've ever done?'

I sighed. 'That's saying something because I've done some *very* stupid things.'

'A lot of people care about you, Rosie. Nan, Kim, your daughter...'

His voice trailed away, and I waited for him to continue.

What about you?

'I know,' I said, breaking the silence. 'I need to be more careful.'

'More than careful. I warned you before about breaking and entering. This time you seemed to think it was fine to be the go-between in a ransom exchange. You were meeting with a dangerous person tonight. Someone who'd already assaulted you. They could have killed you.'

'I was careful.'

'Ring me next time and let me know what's happening.'

I wasn't sure what to say. Had Todd known I was going to meet this guy, he would have stopped me. I was determined to make amends, although I wasn't sure how.

'I've got to sleep,' I said.

'Okay,' he said, and hung up.

Oh dear, I thought. *Todd's really annoyed with me.*

I turned out the light. Trixie settled onto the floor beside my bed. A light breeze pushed against my curtain as I settled back. Even though I expected to fall asleep immediately, my mind kept repeating the last few days' events. The UFO conference. Investigating Hailey and Owen's deaths. Blundering into the Laniakea model. The car containing Owen's body at Elk's Gap. The bridge.

I slept.

The dreams that came were full of me scurrying down the ravine to retrieve the alien relic. It seemed the hill would never end. The closer I got to the bottom, the further away it grew. As I was about to give up, I heard Todd's voice. He was up on the bridge calling my name. I wearily climbed up the ravine to find him waiting.

'I knew this time would come,' he said.

'What do you mean?' I asked.

'This.' Appearing from nowhere was a windowless jail cell.

'I warned you about breaking the law. Now, you're going to jail.'

'No. I'm sorry. I—'

He grabbed my arm and threw me in the cell. As soon as the door had clanged shut, the walls started closing in on me. 'Todd!' I screamed. 'Get me out of here! Please! Help! Get me—'

Drrrrggggg!

My alarm clock exploded in my ear.

'Good grief,' I muttered and opened my eyes to see Trixie staring at me over the end of my bed. 'Morning, girl.'

She panted.

I tested my foot. Although it was painful, the icepack had brought down the swelling. I was lucky, all things considered. Staggering out of bed, I got dressed and was about to take Trixie for a walk when my phone rang: Harry.

'Rosie,' he said. 'Sorry to ring so early. Are you out of bed?'

'Just about to head out.'

'There was a house fire last night in Overside Drive. Can you check it out?'

I frowned. 'Overside Drive? What number?'

'Thirty-four.'

'That's Kylie Crow's house. What happened?'

Harry said he only had the barest of details, and these he'd gotten from listening to emergency services on his police radio scanner. Neighbours had rescued the woman, and she had been taken to Cape Carson hospital. I promised Harry I'd see her.

Within minutes, I was limping into the ward where I found Kylie sitting up in bed. She had a massive lump on her forehead, and her arm was bandaged.

'Rosie!' she said. 'You're the last person I expected to see.'

'I heard about the fire. What happened?'

The woman looked ready to burst into tears. 'I was asleep,' she said. 'About two o'clock, I heard a noise. Before I could put on my bedside lamp, a hand was across my mouth, and I couldn't breathe. Then I felt a terrible pain in my head and passed out.'

'You've been whacked with something. Maybe a bat. Did you get a look at your attacker?'

'No.'

'And what happened then?'

'I awoke sometime later. My hands and feet were bound. A piece of tape was across my mouth. I couldn't move. The living room lamp was on. I could hear someone searching my belongings. My bedroom had been turned upside down, too. I listened as he ransacked the house. Then there was silence.' Tears streamed down the woman's face. 'That was almost the worst part: the silence. My mind went almost crazy imagining what was about to happen.'

I took her hand.

'Then there was a terrible whoosh, and I knew what he'd done. He'd set the house on fire! I screamed and screamed into the gag. At some point, I realised he'd left, and then—more by chance than anything else—the gag came loose, and I yelled at the top of my lungs.'

She explained that the air was choked with smoke and the building was well alight when she heard the front door being smashed down. By then, she had struggled her bonds free and was already making for the front door where a brave neighbour dragged her out.

The woman broke into helpless tears. 'It was a nightmare,' she sobbed. 'An absolute nightmare.'

'The person who broke in,' I said gently. 'Are you sure it was a man?'

Kylie brushed away her tears. 'I don't know,' she admitted. 'I didn't see him. It could have been a woman.'

'Do you keep anything valuable in the house?'

'Not unless you count my romance novel collection.' Again, tears filled her eyes. 'It hasn't quite struck home yet. My house has burnt down. All my things are gone. I don't have my wallet...keys...'

'Kylie,' I said. 'You have to take things one step at a time.' I paused. 'Can you think of who could be responsible?'

She didn't meet my gaze. 'No,' she said, swallowing. 'Why

would anyone do such a thing?'

She was lying. 'Tell me the truth,' I urged. 'Do you know who's behind this?'

'No. I don't know. It's just...I got an odd message recently. Something in the mail. It was so strange I didn't know what to make of it.'

'What did it say?'

She thought. 'It said, *I'm not taking it any longer. Stop or you'll be sorry.*'

The words ran through my mind.

I'm not taking it any longer. Stop or you'll be sorry.

'It arrived in your letterbox?' I asked.

She nodded.

'Why didn't you report it to the police?'

'I thought it was an irate local who hated my books. I write romance. They're not literary novels. Some people hate me simply because I write entertaining books.'

'You need to tell the police about the note.'

She shook her head. 'I can't believe someone would do this simply because of my writing.'

'I don't think it's that at all,' I said. 'Kylie, if you've done something to hurt someone—'

'I haven't done anything—'

'Hailey and Owen are dead. They both received threatening notes, and their notes were similar to yours. Now tell me the truth: who would want to harm you? It could be someone you've hurt, maybe even unintentionally. There must be *some-one*.'

She stared through the hospital window at a tree outside. 'When you mention Hailey and Owen...' she began. 'Plastic Apple wasn't all fun and games. There was nastiness around the group. Vindictive people in it.'

'If one of the members were to cause you harm—'

'It would be Bella.' Kylie hesitated. 'I've never told anyone, but you know the book in Piper's bag? Bella put it there. I saw her do it. While the others were out of the room, I was reading my phone. She was quick, though she may have realised I saw her. That means she probably did all those other horrible things, too.'

'Could she have been the one who assaulted you?'

Kylie shook her head. 'I don't know,' she said. 'I honestly don't know.'

24

Little was left standing of Kylie Crow's home on Overside Drive. Where the pink weatherboard place had stood was now a charred ruin. Some upright posts remained of the bathroom. What had once been the stove and sink lay in a pile of charred metal.

'If it's Bella,' Kim said, 'then she *really* didn't like Kylie.'

I was standing out the front of the house with Kim and Trixie. I gave Trixie an absent pat on the head as I stared at the wreckage. A smoky stench still filled the air. The beautiful garden that had surrounded the place was gone. The front fence had been levelled, probably by the firefighters who had fought the blaze. I snapped a few pictures for the paper before putting my phone away.

'I need coffee,' I said. 'Interested?'

'Have I ever said no?'

'Not often.'

Minutes later, we were seated in the front window of

Sandy's Diner. The bay outside was tranquil and calm, and the horizon a solid sheet of blue. Despite the beautiful surroundings, my emotions were a churning mess.

'This must be linked to Plastic Apple,' I said. 'First Hailey dies, then Owen, and now Kylie is almost murdered and her house burnt down.'

'Plastic Apple should have been named *Poisoned* Apple,' Kim said. 'So who's responsible? Who's the killer?'

I rubbed my chin. 'Jacob was the unofficial president of the club. It's safe to say that he was resentful of Hailey because of her publishing deal. And he seemed to think she got her publishing contract because of her looks. Jacob said she was having a relationship with Bly Simmons.'

'Do you think that's possible?'

'I doubt it. There was a photo of him with another man on his desk, and they looked *very* friendly together. I doubt he had any interest in Hailey.'

'Jacob said that both Owen and Asher were fixated with Hailey. And he said Owen was getting strange calls.'

I nodded. 'A series of anonymous hang-ups,' I said. 'Owen also received that threatening letter after Hailey died: *Stop or you'll regret it.* Soon after, he was murdered and left in the boot of his trunk.'

'Stop what?' Kim asked. 'What was he doing?'

'I don't know, but Hailey and Kylie received similar threats.'

'Did Todd get anything from Owen's vehicle?'

'I'll check with him.' I paused. 'Both Owen and Asher were enamoured with Hailey. Asher was convinced that Owen murdered her.'

Kim bit her lip. 'You know, Owen could have killed Hailey. Kylie said that Asher doted on Hailey. Asher could have been so furious that he then murdered Owen.'

'That's possible. But why would Asher convince us that Owen was Hailey's killer? To divert suspicion from himself, wouldn't he want us to think her death was suicide?'

'That makes sense,' Kim said glumly. 'So, who else do we have?'

'There's Piper. She thought Hailey had put the book in her bag. And she was in love with Owen.'

'Plastic Apple had more love triangles than Jane Austen's collected works,' she said. 'Killing Hailey over a book would be pretty weird. Although, as you say, Piper loved Owen. Maybe she was so unbalanced that she killed Hailey, and when Owen didn't return her affections, she killed him too.'

I nodded. 'There's no fury like a woman scorned,' I said. 'But that doesn't explain the anonymous notes. Whoever sent those notes was furious then and is furious now. So furious that they assaulted Kylie and burned her house down.' I thought. 'Although, it's possible that Kylie's assault isn't real. Kylie was angry with Hailey for not recommending her books to Lancelot Press. After killing Hailey, she may have worried that too many questions were being asked and killed Owen to cover her tracks. When we arrived at her door, she panicked and decided to fake the attack on herself.'

'And destroy her own home?' Kim frowned. 'That's pretty extreme. I think we're forgetting the most obvious suspect of all.'

'The Wicked Witch of the West?'

Kim nodded. 'Bella Lodley. Everyone seemed to think Bella was behind the nasty incidents. Kylie even saw Bella put the book in Piper's bag. And let's not forget the fake letter to Owen from Lancelot.'

'There's something decidedly weird about all that. You could add it to the long list of nasty incidents. Bella could be responsible.'

'Maybe.' Kim glanced at her watch. 'Sorry, but I've got to go. There's a place called the library that pays me money to be there.'

'Their gain. My loss.' I thanked her for meeting up and made my way with Trixie to the Police Station. Jim Turner at the front desk pointed me to Todd's office, where I found him hanging up his phone.

'Hey, Rosie. Are you here to quiz me about evidence? Or have you found another body you neglected to mention earlier.'

'The former, not the latter.'

I sat opposite, and Trixie settled at my knee.

'Okay,' Todd said. 'The UFO relic, or whatever you want to call that thing, is still with forensics, and they should have results back to us in the next day or two.'

'Fair enough. What about Hailey's case?'

'I've had some results, although none of them will make your heart sing. First, the anonymous letters sent to Hailey and Owen. They've been fingerprinted, and the only prints we found belonged to the recipients.'

'So whoever sent the messages wore gloves.'

He nodded. 'And that includes the fake letter from the publisher,' he said. 'Now for the car containing Owen's body. Although there was a mess of prints, the only set the forensics team could identify was Owens. The others are all partials or don't match anyone on record.'

'So that's kind of good news,' I mused. 'If we ever have a suspect...'

'Maybe we can match their prints to the vehicle.'

'What about the weapon used on Owen?'

'We retrieved the bullet. It's a .22 from a hunting rifle or similar.'

I nodded thoughtfully. Forensics could match a bullet to a gun by its striations—the microscopic ridges from the gun barrel. This was good evidence, although we needed the weapon for a match.

It was time to bring him up to speed on the situation with Kylie, so I told him about the anonymous note.

Todd frowned. 'She should have told us earlier.'

'Well, I'm telling you now. These cases are connected. Two people who were members of Plastic Apple are dead, and Kylie has been injured. For all we know, someone is determined to murder all of them.' I glared at him. 'You need to do something about it.'

'All right, Rosie,' he said, nodding. 'Give me the contact details of the other members.'

I handed them over, and Todd spent the next half an hour ringing them. The only one he couldn't contact was Jacob Fobb.

'You're sure this is the right number?' he said.

'Absolutely.'

'Considering what's going on, I think we should go see him.'

I raised an eyebrow. 'We?' I said. 'As in you and me? You're making me feel like I'm a member of the force.'

'Well, you're not, Rosie. That takes training, commitment, and sticking to the rules. The first two, you'd be fine with, but you seem to think rules are merely suggestions.'

'There's a difference?'

I trailed Todd in his cop car through town to Jacob's house. Within minutes, we were knocking on Jacob's front door.

'No answer,' I said to Todd.

Before he could reply, a small truck arrived, and a squat, balding man got out. The truck was emblazoned with *Joe's Pool Cleaning* on the side.

'Jacob's still not home?' he enquired.

'Not by the look of it,' Todd said. 'You were here earlier?'

'I've been waiting half an hour. This is Jacob's usual pool cleaning day. I drove off to get coffee and a bite to eat.'

'This ever happened before?'

'No. And Jacob's picky about that pool because he uses it just about every day.'

Todd nodded glumly and turned to me. 'I think there's an argument that Jacob's safety is in question,' he said. 'Care to join me?'

'I thought you'd never ask.'

Leaving the pool man on the street, we headed to the back door and knocked again. Todd cupped his hands over his eyes so he could see inside. 'Someone's done a number on his house. His kitchen's been wrecked.'

Todd broke down the back door and drew his weapon. We entered to find the entire kitchen had been upended.

'Stay close,' Todd said.

'You'll get no argument from me.'

We cautiously went from room to room. The house was a wreck. Whoever had searched had done a thorough job.

Thousands of papers lay everywhere. They appeared to be Jacob's research on his family. Paintings had been taken off walls. Even the carpet had been pulled up in a few rooms.

'I wonder if they found what they were looking for,' Todd said.

'Who knows,' I replied. 'Hailey, Owen and Kylie's places were searched too, though I have no idea what they're after.'

'And where's Jacob? What's happened to him?'

I remembered Owen's body in the back of his car. He hadn't been found for years. Jacob could have been murdered and his body dumped somewhere. We returned to the kitchen, where Todd peered down at the mess.

'What is this person after?' he murmured. 'Whatever it is, they're not giving up.'

'Uh, Todd.'

'Yeah? What is it?'

I pointed wordlessly. The lap pool wasn't in full view from where we'd entered. From the back window, however, we could see its entire length. Lying face-down on the bottom was Jacob Fobb's body.

25

The afternoon was unseasonably warm.

The police had turned up to help Todd search the property again. The coroner also arrived shortly after, and Jacob's body was removed from the pool. I remembered him talking about his family history. I hoped a family member would retrieve his work and assemble it into something. Then, at least, his efforts would not go to waste.

I was waiting in my car with Trixie. It was after lunch now, and she had fallen asleep on the seat beside me. Despite my stomach grumbling with hunger, I was determined to not leave until I found out the latest.

Todd emerged from the building and arrowed over. 'You're still here?' he said. 'Don't you have a life?'

'Barely. At least there's one positive thing about all this.'

'Which is?'

'It wasn't me finding the body this time.'

Todd sighed. 'True, although I would have preferred to find

Jacob alive.'

'Cause of death? Or is that a silly question?'

'Not too silly. The coroner wants to do a full examination to be sure, but it looks like he was struck over the head—hard. So hard that it fractured his skull. He probably would have died even without being tossed into the pool.'

'And the weapon?'

'Nothing we can see which makes me think the killer brought it with him—and took it away too.'

'Which shows premeditation.' I bit my lip. 'The attack on Kylie Crow means he tried to murder two people last night.'

The cop shook his head. 'I'm stuck for motive,' he said. 'Although there was a lot of animosity in that writers' group, it's hard to believe someone would resort to murder.'

'You never know what's in a person's heart,' I said.

Todd peered at me and smiled sadly. I stared back at him, wondering what was going through his head.

We'd known each other for several months and, apart from a brief goodnight kiss at the end of the night, nothing more had happened between us.

I should say something, I thought. *Why can't I say how I feel?*

Taking a deep breath, I was about to blurt out that something—anything—when Todd's phone rang. He stepped away and answered the call. When he returned, he said, 'There's a car fatality out on Millicent Drive. I'd better get moving.'

'What about the other members of Plastic Apple?'

'I've warned them to be on guard. They can ring us if they see anything suspicious.

He returned to his car and drove away. I turned to Trixie. 'What am I going to do?' I asked her. 'I think I'm kinda in love with that guy.' Trixie snuggled her head against my arm. 'I know *you* love me. I just wish I knew about him.'

I headed down to the bay and parked the car. Taking Trixie with me, I made my way along the coastal path and up the hill to Cut Rock Lookout. A breeze had picked up during the morning. Now it was blowing hard.

Reaching the lookout, I peered out at the boundless ocean. The tops of waves had turned white, and the cold air stung my eyes. Coming here always helped me to think, and now I needed to think more than ever.

Only four members of Plastic Apple remained: Asher Vorback, Piper Ellis, Kylie Crow, and Bella Lodley. One of them had to be the killer, and it had to relate back to books and publishing. I ran through the details in my mind. Hailey had been offered a publishing deal, and the group's reaction had been far from positive.

Some felt slighted. Others were furious. It seemed the same publisher had also been interested in Owen's book, or books, although that offer wasn't genuine. What was the purpose of sending him a fake letter? And what had happened to Owen's writing?

I had a lot of questions and no answers. There was someone who had known the group back in the day, and that was Ian Westlok. The owner of Unicorn Books had probably seen the group every time they met. And they still continued to visit the store. I returned to my jeep with renewed enthusiasm and drove to the bookshop.

Ian was at the counter with several customers lined up. Not wanting to bother him, I continued on through the building. I inhaled deeply. There was nothing like the comforting smell of books to set the mind at ease. Maybe it was all those stories and wisdom they contained.

If I recreated what it was like for the members of Plastic Apple, a random neuron in my brain might fire and give me some answers. First, I'd start with the cellar. That was where they were supposed to hold their meeting.

As I descended to the empty room, the old timber stairs creaked under my weight. Ian had said this was the least used room in the shop, which is why he let Plastic Apple meet here. My eyes took in the bookshelves and the old brick walls behind. Could something be hidden in here? Maybe in one of the books? Or could Owen's manuscripts be jammed behind the bookcases?

Scrambling up onto a small footstool, I peered into the tiny gap behind the shelves. Nothing. There was barely enough room for a dozen pages, let alone several full manuscripts. And Owen had handwritten his books. They would be enormous. I examined the volumes on the top shelves; they hadn't been touched for years. Even I could tell they would never sell. They were dusty tomes that were decades out of date. Ian could have thrown them away, but he needed something up there.

I checked under the timber stairs. Here was another squat bookshelf with a small sign on the top that read *Einstein's Corner*. Below was a quote attributed to the great man himself:

We cannot solve our problems with the same thinking we used when we created them.

It gave me something to think about as I returned to the middle of the room. Finally, I checked under the table and chairs. Again, nothing.

But the last meeting of Plastic Apple wasn't held here because of the April Fool's Day quake. Maybe I was searching in the wrong place. I returned upstairs. That last infamous meeting had been held in the cookbook room.

Fortunately, this room was empty too. It was a similar configuration to downstairs, but with fewer chairs. And these were lounge chairs. The type of comfortable chair you sunk into with a good book and a cup of hot chocolate. Hours might pass while you sat here reading.

My eyes scanned the shelves, taking in various titles: *Easy Italian for Beginners, French Patisserie, Thai Cooking in Ten*

Minutes.

This was where it had all happened. Where everyone had unleashed their long-held resentments. I started another search. The configuration of this room was similar to the cellar, although it was larger with taller shelves. Like the room downstairs, the uppermost shelf carried dead stock, and there was a gap between the shelf and the roof.

Fortunately, there was a footstool in here, too, so I climbed up and felt in the narrow gap of one shelf.

Dust, dust, and more dust.

Which was hardly surprising, really. I wouldn't dust up there, either. I continued searching along the top of the rest of the shelves.

Nothing. Zilch. Zero.

I hadn't felt this frustrated for a long time. My eyes scanned the shelves again.

There had to be something in here. Something I'd missed. My gaze settled on one of the top shelves. A couple of books were sticking out. Not far. Just a few centimetres. Climbing onto the footstool again, I dragged out the books and reached in. At first, nothing, and then—

My fingers raked along the edge of a hard object. There was a scrape of plastic and a jangle of metal. Then I had the objects in my hand.

A set of keys and a mobile phone.

An *old* mobile phone.

What are these doing here?

Judging by the dust, they'd been here for years. Something clicked in my mind. Both Asher Vorback's phone and keys had gone missing three years ago. He lost his phone at the last meeting, and keys at one shortly before that. He'd had to walk home after the meeting.

Someone put these here.

And then, in a sudden blinding flash of realisation, it all came together.

26

'Am I late?' Piper asked.

'Just in time,' I assured her. 'Grab a seat in the café. We're starting shortly.'

Todd, Kim, and I were in the doorway of the Unicorn Bookshop with Constable Turner.

I'd asked for the shop to be shut. Despite the shop's marketing motto—*We Never Close*—Ian had reluctantly acquiesced. He sat at the counter, sorting old books while surreptitiously watching everyone assembled around the café tables.

Piper scooted past us and took a seat with the others.

'It's a good thing I like you, Rosie,' Todd said. 'Because no other cop in their right mind would allow this.'

Kim spoke up. 'I know what you mean,' she said. 'Rosie's left me in the dark too.'

'Never fear,' I said mysteriously. 'All will become clear soon enough. Todd, just be ready for anything.'

They were all here: Bella Lodley, Asher Vorback, Kylie Crow

and Piper Ellis. Kylie had been discharged from hospital. Apart from a bandage on her head, she looked well, if not a little uncomfortable. The others looked uncomfortable, too, which was understandable. Todd had virtually demanded that they attend this meeting.

'Well,' I said. 'We may as well get this show on the road.'

Todd and Constable Turner remained at the door as Kim took a seat, and I crossed to the café counter and leaned against it. 'Thanks for coming,' I said. 'Especially at such short notice.'

'What else could we do?' Kylie said. 'The cops told us to come. Said our lives were in danger.'

'I heard about Jacob,' Bella said. 'Simply dreadful news.' She glared at Todd. 'I hope you're working on finding the killer. Jacob was a fine man.'

'And the third member of Plastic Apple to die,' Asher said. 'I understand that Owen's body was found recently. There's a madman on the loose.'

'Do you think he's after us?' Piper asked.

'I promise you'll all be safe after today,' I said. 'Although it took me a while, I finally worked out what this was all about.' I reached into my pocket and produced a plastic evidence bag containing the keys and phone. 'Asher, I believe these are yours.'

He peered at them, frowning. 'My goodness,' he said. 'I think they are. Where did you get them?'

'They were hidden behind some books in the cookbook room. They've been there for years. Three years, I believe. Ever since they were stolen from you.'

'Stolen.' Asher repeated the word as if it were in a foreign language. 'So I didn't lose them. They were taken.'

'Who took them?' Bella asked.

I hesitated. 'Before I answer that,' I said, 'I want to take us back to that last meeting of Plastic Apple. You'd been meeting for years, helping each other to become writers. From what everyone's said to me, the group was helpful but also terribly dysfunctional. There wasn't a lot of love shared. Kim said the name Poisoned Apple would have been more appropriate.'

'That's a big harsh,' Kylie said.

I ignored her. 'A lot happened in those last few meetings,' I continued. 'You discovered that Hailey could be signing a publishing deal. That caused all kinds of animosity.'

'Only because she didn't write the book,' Bella said. 'The rest of us contributed so much that it was barely hers anymore.'

'And she had the cheek to call it her own,' Asher added. 'No wonder we were annoyed.'

I went on. 'A string of nasty things happened in those last few months,' I said. 'The mirror on Jacob's car was damaged, and he received an email containing a virus. Asher's keys went missing. Later, so did his phone. A book ended up in Piper's bag. Hailey's dog died. Several of Kylie's novels in the library were vandalised.'

'And nothing terrible happened to either Owen or Bella,' Piper said, her eyes not meeting Bella's glare. 'Nothing.'

'Actually, something *really* nasty happened to Owen. He received a letter from Lancelot Press telling him they were interested in his writing. Can you imagine that? The pleasure of finding that a publisher is interested in your book? But then, learning that the letter is a fake? It's not real? How disappointing that would have been. The only saving grace of that horrible act is that Owen never discovered the truth. He received the letter but hadn't gotten around to checking its veracity. He died before he could contact Lancelot.' I paused. 'But you are right about something, Piper. Nothing terrible happened to Bella.' My gaze moved across the room, finally settling on her. 'Nothing.'

'I was lucky.' The scowling woman's voice was hoarse. 'Are you suggesting those accidents had something to do with me? How are you—'

'*How dare I?*' I snapped. 'You evil woman. You have no idea what you set in motion.'

'What are you talking about?'

I scowled at her. 'Let's go back to that last meeting: the day when Hailey naively announced with much excitement that she was receiving a sizable amount for her book. You all reacted with resentment. Everyone except Owen. He was in love with

Hailey, and he—at least—was happy for her.

'But let's go back a little further. That last meeting was on the ground floor in the cookbook room. It wasn't your usual place. It's smaller with fewer chairs. Actually, it only has four chairs.' I swallowed. 'And that's what clicked with me in the end: *the number of chairs*. Piper even told us that people went searching for more on the day of the last meeting.

'Your usual meetings were normally held downstairs. There are seven chairs in the cellar, but Ian had asked you not to go down there. The earthquake had caused damage the day before. But one of you went down there.' I paused. 'That was you, wasn't it, Asher?'

The little man swallowed hard. 'Me? No...I...'

'I'm sure there was a barrier across the top of the stairs, but you ignored it and headed down. It would only take a moment. There must have been quite a mess, although rather than grabbing some chairs and heading back up, you decided to examine the damage. One of the walls had been cracked.' I stopped. 'You must have received a terrible shock when you peered into the crack—and staring back at you was the mummified body of Lynette Westlok.'

Kim's mouth dropped. 'The—*what*?'

'Everyone thought Lynette had left town with another man,' I continued. 'At least, that's what Ian told us. But that wasn't the truth. After years of marriage, she'd had enough.

She wanted out. But Ian didn't want that. No, his wife wasn't walking out on him, taking half the business, and destroying everything they'd built up.

'People in town weren't that close to Lynette. Partly, it was because she and Ian had spent so many hours building the Unicorn Bookshop into a success.

'And Lynette was an orphan. She didn't have family who would wonder what had happened to her. So, not many people asked questions when Lynette 'left town'. I know I didn't. People weren't shocked. Surprised, maybe. But not shocked. Ian is such a pleasant man. So helpful. No one could imagine him hurting anyone, let alone *murdering* his wife.'

All eyes were on Ian Westlok now. He was sitting very still and had stopped sorting books. He simply gazed back at me, his face unreadable. He could have been a statue.

'Four years ago, Ian had to do major repairs to the cellar. This involved replacing one of the walls. This work was still in progress when Lynette announced she was leaving. Ian killed her. But then what could he do? He had to dispose of the body, and the easiest way to do that was to brick her up behind the wall. He told the story about Lynette running off to Queensland with another man. It was a clever explanation. Everyone believed him, and he continued with his life. No one knew that his wife's corpse was hidden behind the cellar wall.

'It was the earthquake a year later that brought him unstuck.

It was April Fool's Day, the day before Plastic Apple held their April meeting. The quake caused minor damage right through the area, including the new wall in the cellar. It created an enormous crack. He couldn't close the shop. That would seem too strange. After all, the shop's slogan was: *We Never Close.* The best Ian could do was to shut that room for the day and move Plastic Apple into the cookbook room on ground level.

'It was Asher who ignored the chain and went down to find more chairs. Out of curiosity, he must have peered into the crack—and that's when he saw the body of Lynette Westlok. At first, it was a terrible shock, but then he saw an opportunity. He knew something that no one else did. Ian had murdered his wife and bricked her up behind the wall. Surely there was money to be made.'

I turned to Asher. 'You took some pictures of Lynette with your phone,' I said, 'and you cut off a piece of her bloodied shirt. That evidence was going to make you money. A lot of money. That's when you began blackmailing Ian. I'm not sure how much it was. Probably not a fortune, I imagine. You didn't want to kill the golden goose. All you wanted to do was slowly bleed it dry.'

Asher had turned white. 'No,' he said. 'None of this is true...none...'

Todd spoke up. 'We've looked at the phone.' Asher clamped his mouth shut. 'We've seen the photos.'

I said, 'Ian was in a panic when he received the demand for money. It was too late to move the body. Someone out there had incriminating photos and the bloodied fabric.'

'I'd get the demand for more money,' Ian said. His voice was calm and measured. 'And a tiny square of her shirt.'

I turned to him. 'You needed to find the blackmailer,' I said. 'The moment you remembered the extra chairs in the cookbook room, you knew it had to be a member of Plastic Apple. Who would have gone down there? Your first thought was Hailey. You'd heard she was coming into money and planning a holiday to Europe.'

'I sent her a note and got no response.'

'We found that note.'

He nodded. 'I just wanted to talk to her,' he said. 'She was surprised when I turned up at her house. The conversation started normally enough, but then I blurted it all out. I lost my temper and started screaming at her. Suddenly she was on the ground and...' He clenched his jaw. 'That's how it was with Lynette. She wanted to leave, but I told her she couldn't, and everything went fuzzy. And then she was dead.' Ian sighed. 'Anyway, Hailey was unconscious, and I had to do something.'

'So you carried her body to the top of the cliff,' I said, 'and threw her over. Then you returned to the house, wrote the suicide note, and searched. Not finding the evidence must have been terrible. Now you were in a double-panic. Not only had you murdered both your wife and Hailey, but you couldn't find the incriminating evidence.

'Still, you may have thought you might be all right. The pictures weren't on her phone. Maybe she'd deleted them, and if the remains of the bloody shirt turned up, who would even know what it was? There was no reason for anyone to connect it to Lynette.'

A sad smile appeared on Ian's lips. 'For a while, I thought I was safe. I had a few weeks of reprieve. Then the next letter arrived. The moment I received it, I knew I was wrong. Hailey wasn't the blackmailer.'

'So then you suspected Owen.'

'He was a big strong man with a violent past, and less than ethical. I knew some of his history, so I thought it had to be him. I sent him a threatening letter and got no response, so I followed him one day and got lucky. He was on a drive to Elk's Gap. I forced him off the road and confronted him.' Ian stopped as if peering into the past. 'I had the gun in my hand, and Owen was staring at me as if I'd gone mad. He had no idea what I was talking about. I realised I'd made another terrible mistake, so I...I did what I had to do.'

You murdered him, I thought. *And dumped his car and body in the bush.*

'I gave in after that,' Ian continued. 'I just paid the money. You have no idea what a nightmare it's been. Every month another demand for cash would arrive. It's a terrible thing to be under the thumb of someone. To be slowly crushed like a bug. I had no idea who the blackmailer could be. The ex-members of Plastic Apple would come into the shop, and I would watch them, wondering, *Are you the blackmailer?* His eyes fixed on Asher. 'Strangely, I didn't suspect you. I didn't think you had it in you to concoct such an evil plan.'

Asher had turned dead white. 'I...I don't...'

Ian smiled sadly. 'I don't hate you, Asher. You blackmailed me for three years, but the Hell I created was in my own mind. Every day I've tortured myself with the same thoughts: *Why didn't I let Lynette leave? Why did I have to kill her?*

'Asher didn't even have his phone,' I said. 'Like his keys, it had been stolen and hidden as a cruel joke. He was bluffing when he said he had the pictures. You could have called his bluff and not paid a cent.'

Ian laughed. It wasn't his usual jolly laugh that we'd come to know over the years. It was tinged with hysteria and sadness and—yes—relief. It was over. He was undone, and now the guilt he had carried could finally be lifted.

As far as Asher was concerned, the man had turned pasty white during my denouement. He may not have known that Hailey's death and Owen's disappearance were caused by Ian. Those events could have been a tragic coincidence. But the penny had to drop after Owen's body was found and Kylie was attacked. The icing on the cake had to be Jacob's murder. Then he knew the lengths Ian Westlok would go to track down the blackmailer.

Todd and Constable Turner stepped forward. By then, Ian's laughter had stopped. The expression on his face was the same one we knew and loved. The same smile that had lulled us into believing he couldn't hurt a fly.

He went quietly with Constable Turner. As for Asher, the little man wept and struggled, and Todd had to call in two other constables to drag him away.

After they were gone, a long silence settled over the room. Everyone sat alone with their own thoughts. This had been a lot to take in.

'Rosie,' Kim said, finally breaking the quiet. 'There's something I still don't understand: Owen's books. What happened to his novels?'

'Oh, yes,' I said softly. 'I wondered about that too. Then I remembered that the only person Bella seemed to like was Owen.'

Bella glared at me. 'What are you saying?'

'You were in love with Owen.'

'How ridiculous! I was old enough to be his mother!'

'Which wouldn't matter if that's all it was,' I said. 'But your interest went beyond that. After Owen's disappearance, you broke into his house.'

The woman looked ready to attack me. '*You stupid woman*!' she screeched. 'I don't need to stay here—'

'No, you don't,' I agreed. 'But the truth may as well come out. Maybe Owen rejected you, or maybe you finally realised he would never return your affections. The woman he loved was Hailey. You sent the letter pretending to be from the publisher. You did it to hurt him. But after his disappearance, you began thinking about his books. Owen had thousands of pages. And you knew his work was good. It was popular fiction. Not to your taste, but that made no difference. Not where money was concerned—'

'This is idiotic—'

'But you didn't care. Owen was gone, likely dead, and *someone* may as well benefit. And why not you? So you broke in and stole his writing. I'm sure you changed all the character's names and places. And no one else in Plastic Apple read sword and sorcery novels. They would never know. So, you typed up his books and sent them to a publisher. It must have come as a surprise when they were accepted, and the money came flooding in. You had to keep your name hidden, but that made no difference. Although you were wealthy before, now you were rich and that's all that mattered.'

'You're wrong. It's all lies—'

'You've always liked crossword puzzles, Bella, but that love of puzzles extends to anagrams. Doesn't it?'

Bella had turned scarlet with rage. Now her face paled until only two bright red blotches of colour were in her cheeks, and her eyes were wide. Wide with realisation that everything she'd built was about to come unstuck.

'No,' Bella gasped. 'No, I—'

'We noticed those books on your shelf by those fantasy authors. Tolkien, Le Guin, and others. Some were by Ally Bolleed, a new author who's done well over the last few years. You said reading fantasy novels had become a guilty pleasure. If only that were true.

'No, I—'

I glared at her. 'You love laughing at others behind their backs, but you're not as clever as you think,' I said. 'With some rearranging, it's obvious that *Ally Bolleed* is an anagram for *Bella Lodley*.'

The tears began to stream down Bella's cheeks. 'I didn't know they'd be so successful,' she cried. 'I didn't mean to hurt anyone.'

There was ice in my voice as I continued. 'It's okay, Bella,' I said. 'I'll personally make sure that Owen gets the recognition he deserves. I'm sure everything you've made will go to his father. That's only right. Bert Stamett will finally learn how great his son truly was. The publicity from your despicable act will probably make Owen's books more popular than ever.'

27

'Are you sure about this?' Todd asked.

'It's the only thing that makes sense,' I replied.

We were in the lobby of the Kilkenny Arms. It was early the next day, and Todd had arranged to return the relic to Barry, Neo, and Jasper. The elevator door opened, the trio emerged and arrowed over.

Jasper saw the bag in Todd's hand. 'Thank goodness,' he said. 'You've brought it with you.'

'I'm surprised.' Neo frowned suspiciously at Todd. 'The police are government agents. I would have expected you to file it away in an underground laboratory.'

'That's too much hard work,' Todd said dryly. 'I looked up your so-called relic on the internet and found it's actually an intake manifold for a car. Looks like someone used a vice to twist it out of shape.'

Barry's jaw dropped. 'That ridiculous,' he spluttered. 'It came off a flying saucer. It's from the Blackwood crash.'

'Then alien spaceships run on V8 engines.' He nodded to the bar. 'Let's sit. We need to talk.'

The others followed us uncertainly into the bar. It was quiet at this time of day, so we grabbed a table near the window. Todd nodded to the door. It had been empty before, but now two constables stood there waiting.

'What's this all about?' Neo asked.

'Nothing for you to worry about,' I told her. 'By the way, I was able to do some research on that house next to the Blackwood forest. A family was living there, and it seems they did disappear—to the Northern Territory. Their name was Bergmann, not Berman, hence the difficulty in tracking them down. They moved out the same week as the UFO sighting. I found them on Facebook. They look like lovely people.'

'Clones,' Jasper said, shaking his head sadly. 'Or possibly aliens wearing human skin.'

'Anyway,' Todd said, keen to move on. 'We had the, er, relic analysed and found something incriminating.'

'Which was?' Barry asked.

'The only fingerprints we found on it were yours.'

'Well?' Barry said, forcing a laugh. 'What a stupid thing to say! Of course, the only prints on it were mine.'

'So that makes sense to you?'

'Certainly!'

'Barry,' I said patiently. 'Why were no one else's prints on it?'

His gaze zig-zagged between Todd and me. 'Rosie.' Barry's jaw hardened. 'I can understand government agents working against us. But I would have thought better of you.' He gathered himself up. 'I will remind you that the relic was in my safekeeping for years. I have been *the keeper of the relic*. The only person who has ever handled it is me.'

'True.' Silence settled over the table before I continued. 'So the only fingerprints on it should have been yours. Except, I grabbed the relic when I found it at that abandoned house on Crescent Drive. I picked it up, so my fingerprints should be on it.' I paused. 'That's really why I wanted Todd to have it examined. Not to check for your prints, or anyone else's, but to check for *mine*.' I let all this settle in. 'How can it be that my prints aren't on it?'

'Because it's a copy,' Jasper fumed, understanding. 'It's not real.'

I continued. 'And you can understand the extortionist swapping out the real item for a fake,' I said. 'The fake would then be wiped clean as a whistle. But if that's the case, how can Barry's prints be on it? There can only be one possible explanation: the extortionist swapped it for the one I manhandled. And if Barry's prints are on it then—'

'He's the extortionist,' Neo said.

'No...' Barry said. 'I...a conspiracy...they're lying...'

'You extorted fifty thousand dollars from AFSA,' I said.

'I'm guessing your wife is your accomplice. As you reminded me on that first day, she was once the face of Hairy Harold's Motorcycles.'

'She *does* ride a motorcycle,' Jasper said, turning to Barry. 'Why did you do it? After all these years? Why?'

Barry Rycroft stared wordlessly at the others before finally cracking. 'I had to,' he wailed. 'My business is in trouble. I'm about to lose everything. I desperately needed the money—'

Todd nodded to the two constables in the doorway, who handcuffed him, and led him away.

'What will happen to him?' Neo asked. 'And his wife, Elsa?'

'Jail,' Todd said. 'For extortion and the assault on Rosie.'

Jasper looked lost. 'Everything's gone wrong,' he said. 'The conference has been a disaster. Our president's been arrested. Our reputation's in tatters. Now we'll have a court case that could go on for months. Or years.' His eyes turned to me. 'AFSA needs a new president. I was thinking of applying, but I've had second thoughts.'

'What do you mean?' I asked.

'Will you do it?' he pleaded. 'Having a true believer in the media would go a long way.'

'I'm sure it would,' I agreed as Todd, and I stood. 'But AFSA is better off in your hands than it ever would be in mine. Although forces are working against us, you know what you must do.' I paused dramatically. '*Watch the skies.*'

I gave them one last nod before leaving with Todd. Once we'd reached the footpath, he turned to me. '*Watch the skies?*' he said. 'That's so corny. I can't believe you just said that.'

'Hey, it's a big universe.' I shrugged. 'Kim told me she saw a UFO, and I believe her. I don't know if it was a flying saucer. It was a UFO—an unidentified flying object—and it remains unidentified. Maybe flying saucers are visiting Earth. Who knows? I haven't seen one. I'm just a reporter working for a small-town newspaper.' I nodded in the direction of the bay. 'Feel like a walk?'

We strolled down to the beach. It was a beautiful day. With both conferences finished, Cape Carson would soon return to normal.

'By the way,' Todd said. 'I bumped into Nan the other day, and she said she'd been asked to stand as President for AFSA. The other AFSA, I mean.'

'Oh yes, I know. Nan's turned them down.'

'Really?'

'Nan says it's full of old people.'

Todd grinned. 'Well, she wouldn't want that.'

We continued walking. I glanced at Todd after a while. There was something I had to say and it couldn't wait.

'Todd,' I said. 'Are we still friends?'

He looked at me with surprise. 'Of course, we are.'

'I know you were annoyed about me breaking into the house

on Crescent Drive—'

'And the ransom exchange at The Huxley Bridge.'

'—and that too,' I said. 'I promise I will be more respectful of the law from now on.' I paused. 'It's just that when I start investigating a mystery, I can't seem to stop! It's like I can't give up until everything is resolved. Until I've got all the answers!'

Todd started to laugh.

'What?' I said. 'What so funny?'

'Sorry,' he said. 'It's just that there's one mystery you didn't solve.'

'Which is?'

'Neo.' He leaned close. 'Her real name is Olive Snell-munkle.'

'Olive Snellmunkle?' I suppressed a smile. 'Goodness. I wonder why she changed it to Neo?'

But the adventure doesn't end here!

Catch Rosie's next mystery in:

Cats, Castles and Murder!

ABOUT THE AUTHOR

Darrell Pitt is a prolific author, with more than two dozen novels in print. Writing for both young and old alike, Darrell's books traverse multiple genres including cozy mysteries, science-fiction and adventure stories. A proud resident of Melbourne, Australia, Darrell shares his home with his wife and says he owns too many books (as if such a thing were possible!)

His literary journey began with a passion for crafting short stories in his youth, eventually evolving into full-length novels. Among his accolades, "A Toaster on Mars" earned a prestigious spot on the shortlist for the 2017 Russell Prize, showcasing Darrell's unique brand of humour. His novel, "The Firebird Mystery", received commendation from The Children's Book Council of Australia as a Notable book in 2015.

Darrell's Teen Superhero series has garnered widespread acclaim, while his Rosie Ryan books are a series of delightful mysteries set in a distinctly Australian environment. Among the books he's currently working on are a tech-thriller, a time-travel novel, and a mystery book set in 1960's Victoria.